They Will Have Visions and Dreams

They Will Have Visions and Dreams

FAITH DAEHLIN

TATE PUBLISHING
AND ENTERPRISES, LLC

Published by Tate Publishing & Enterprises, LLC
127 E. Trade Center Terrace | Mustang, Oklahoma 73064 USA
1.888.361.9473 | www.tatepublishing.com

Tate Publishing is committed to excellence in the publishing industry. The company reflects the philosophy established by the founders, based on Psalm 68:11,
"The Lord gave the word and great was the company of those who published it."

Book design copyright © 2012 by Tate Publishing, LLC. All rights reserved.
Cover design by Lauro Talibong
Interior design by Mary Jean Archival

Published in the United States of America

ISBN: 978-1-62147-216-2
1. Fiction / Christian / General
2. Fiction / Romance / Paranormal
12.10.17

Dedication

This book is dedicated to those I love.
You know who you are.

Prologue

Little blond curls peeked out from under the covers of the bed nearest the window, but no face responded to the alarm clock's buzz.

Grace rose from her own bed and pulled a worn bathrobe around her slender, adolescent frame. Pushing her sleep-tousled hair away from her face, she stepped lightly over to her sister's bedside and gently turned back a corner of the blanket. Her shoulder-length hair, its red highlights glinting in the morning sun streaming through the window, fell back around her face as she leaned over to give her sister a gentle kiss on the forehead. "Come on, Bunny," she urged, "let's start the day the right way."

Wide-set, round eyes opened slowly, reluctantly.

"You know, the right way, the *O* way, the get up and—"

From another room, a slamming door followed by a loud angry curse shattered the morning's stillness. Grace sighed. She loved the freshness and purity of morning. Mornings seemed to have a way of letting one start over all new, the mistakes and misdeeds of the previous day swept away by the light of dawn. Now this morning had a blot already.

Grace could remember a quiet morning, but that had been quite a while ago. These days both morning and evening were likely to be punctuated by shouts and curses, sneering accusations, arguments, crying, the sound of breaking objects, or worst of all, the thud of her mother's body hitting the wall as her latest live-in boyfriend—little different from the last one—beat up on her. Right now it sounded as though he had been on another of his all-night binges and had just come home, again turning the kitchen into a battleground.

Seven-year-old Bunny winced at the sound and hunched deeper into the bed, resisting the wake-up call. She just stared up at her big sister, her eyes reflecting both sadness and apprehension as she pulled the blanket back up over her ears. Grace sighed. She wished she could change things for them. She understood why Bunny didn't really want to wake up and get out of bed. And it just didn't seem fair to be so young and not want to face the day. She smoothed back the hair that had fallen across Bunny's forehead and smiled wryly. "Just another day at the Fairchilds'," Grace said. Sometimes that brought a smile despite the tension, but not today.

Grace let it go for the moment and turned to get dressed. As she pulled on her clothes and combed her hair, she considered how there were not only fewer and fewer smiles in the morning from Bunny, but in fact, there was a growing lack of enthusiasm for anything at all in the little girl's life. Sadly, Grace remembered what a bouncy, happy toddler Bunny had been, full of energy and curiosity and outgoing almost to a fault. Stifling the urge to sigh again, Grace tied her sneakers, grabbed her and her sister's backpacks, and headed for the kitchen. Perhaps she could quiet things down a bit in the kitchen before her sister got there too.

The snarly exchange stopped as Grace walked in. She knew better than to say anything cheerful. From experience, she knew a vague smile and nod with no direct eye contact with anyone would work best to avoid simply becoming a new target for loaded words. She walked in like a soldier on a mission and started looking for something she could make for breakfast. Sometimes this was the first big challenge of the day. This morning there were a few pieces of bread in a bag on the counter and a tiny bit of butter in an extremely crummy dish next to the toaster. That would have to do.

Warm toast placed on a piece of notebook paper—there were no napkins to be found—almost completed the mission. By the time Bunny entered the kitchen, Grace had schoolbooks, breakfast, and good-byes ready. Taking her little sister's hand, she all but ran out of the house and down the street, pulling Bunny along with her. *Mission complete.*

⊰|⊱

School was a place of respite for both girls. They prospered in its relatively ordered calm, and both enjoyed the often-interesting challenges of class. In fact, school had become even better for Bunny since the teachers had stopped trying to make her talk like other children.

Grace knew she *thought* lots of things, but Bunny had not spoken out loud since she was three or four, when one evening Ma had been beaten up right in front of Bunny's terrified eyes. Worse yet, the incident had been triggered by something Bunny herself said.

All she had done was ask for the syrup to go with the hot cakes they were having for supper. But when the bottle turned out to be almost empty, their mother's boyfriend had reacted loudly and angrily, accusing Ma of never having enough food in the house and not being a good cook either, not even a good mother. The more he shouted, the worse his behavior became, until he was throwing food then plates then their mother herself around the kitchen.

Since that night, their mother had pleaded, cajoled, and even threatened, but Bunny just wouldn't speak. Grace had a theory, whether it was correct or not, that Bunny *believed* it was her fault Ma had been beaten. Grace thought it was kind of ironic that she and Ma had called her little sister Bunny, and now she wouldn't make a sound—just like a little rabbit.

⊰|⊱

Grace sighed as her thoughts returned to the school work at hand. She and Bunny had built a lot of love into their quiet relationship. She refused to think about this morning's sour start and just hoped the argument had been resolved by the time they returned home after school. She then put pencil to paper and embraced the orderly cleanliness of her scholastic environment.

Grace would always remember the exact angle of the sun as they headed home from school that day and the patterns of shadow and light it made on the road as it came through the trees.

At afternoon dismissal time, the girls met as usual by the front steps of the school. Grace took a few minutes to look at Bunny's drawings and other papers from the school day, praising Bunny for the good job she had done. Then, after putting the papers away, helping Bunny put on her backpack, and shouldering her own, Grace headed them for home. On the way, she pointed out the squirrels playing in the trees and tried to get Bunny to at least join her in kicking and scuffling through the crunchy autumn leaves that were piling up beside the road. But the closer to home they got, the stiller Bunny became.

It was pretty much the same as any other day. However, this day as they came around the corner nearest their house, Grace saw the yellow tape around their yard and stopped, pulling Bunny close to her side as if shielding her from an oncoming speeding car. Grace turned, moving Bunny away from the view of all the people going in and out of their home.

The local police car sat at an odd angel out front, as if Sheriff Tom hadn't bothered to actually park at all. A lot of the neighbors were outside their houses. In fact, it looked as though half the town was present, standing in yards and spilling into the road. Here and there a couple stood together, men's arms protectively around their wives or hands held in mutual comfort. In addition, a collection of bikes and skateboards lay beside the road, and the adults in the yards nearest the girls' home seemed to be forming a wall to press back the growing crowd of children just coming home from school.

Strangers with cameras and others with little notebooks and pens were crowding in front of Grace and Bunny's house, pressing up against the tape. What looked like a white van was parked in the driveway on the other side of the house, its rear end just visible from where the girls stood. Others—a man carrying a black satchel and some uniformed officers carrying brown paper sacks—could be seen leaving the house, getting into cars, and driving away. For Grace, the scene was in slow motion, every detail and movement and color burning itself into her memory. As she and her little sister stood inconspicuously in the shade of one of the neighbor's oak trees, a man carrying the end of a stretcher started backing out of their front door.

At the same moment, a neighbor and his wife both happened to look over to the place where the girls stood rooted to the spot. The couple exchanged a confused, sort of panicked look, and with almost one mind, they both turned and walked quickly toward the girls. The closer they came to Grace and Bunny, the more they blocked Grace's view of the scene. Grace jerked to the side to verify her glimpse of a red-stained white sheet, but the neighbor man gently put his thick, hairy arm around her and turned her away. Grace strained to peek over his shoulder and saw that the man's wife had hunched down, almost surrounding Bunny with her plump frame, and was whispering something into Bunny's ear.

Grace didn't like the out-of-control feeling she was experiencing as the man ushered them toward the house next door. She felt a deep need to be outside, to sort out the confusion of the happenings. But once Bunny was gently led into the neighbor's house, Grace followed them in and sat quietly at the kitchen table with Bunny as the woman busily put cookies on a chipped china plate and set them on the table then started pouring milk into large tumblers. With raised eyebrows, she held up a cold beer, silently questioning her husband as he took a seat with the girls, but when he shook his head, she put it back in the refrigerator and sat down with the others. Grace noticed the woman had one leg that seemed a little stiff, an odd detail branded into her memory.

The girls locked eyes across the table. The woman looked at the man, but the man was staring at the table and running his hand through his not-so-clean, wavy hair. Turning away from Bunny, Grace just sat still, looking at the man and waiting for more information.

Then he cleared his throat a tiny bit, and when he raised his eyes to look at his wife, Grace noticed that they seemed unusually moist. Most definitely, something big had happened while they were at school—something bad. Many scenarios sped through Grace's mind: more fighting, Ma got hurt, her boyfriend hurt himself while drunk, someone else had an accident. The man started speaking so softly that Grace barely heard him. Indeed, it was Bunny's widening eyes that drew Grace's attention to what he was saying.

"…think she didn't make it, and when he found himself trapped by the cops…they tried to talk him into surrendering…long time…he just shot himself. There's no mistake, he's gone, but her, now…" His words trailed off.

Like an explosion, Grace was out of her chair, out the door, and across the lawn to her own house just in time to see the white van, actually an ambulance, pulling away from the curb and rolling down the road without the lights on. Grace ran after it. She ran faster than ever before, and she could hear someone shouting loudly right next to her. It seemed that a very loud and upset person was running with her, running behind the big white ambulance, shouting.

As the ambulance picked up speed, she couldn't run any faster to keep up, and the whole thing slowed down again, until she realized it was she who had been shouting. She awkwardly slowed her legs down and stopped in the road, arms hanging and chest heaving, with clouds of dust settling in the dreamlike twilight.

Standing there, she replayed the ambulance's departure in her mind again. They had not used the emergency lights. She was sure of that. Deep inside she knew her mother was dead.

Her body was turning and walking back toward the crowd of onlookers, familiar and unfamiliar—and Bunny. Adult faces looked at her with pity, but inside she was already shutting down her grief. As she straightened her shoulders, her mind began turning over plans and decisions that had to be made.

She felt old, much older than eleven.

1

Anyone could tell that the attractive, teenage blonde with the cherubic face standing by the steps of the university's administration building was looking for someone. She moved her head back and forth, her eyes searching the flowing crowd as streams of students poured out of classroom buildings and the library like merging rivers, filling the walkways and moving toward dorms, parking lots, and streets.

"Hey, hottie," called out one of the passersby, "how 'bout goin' out with me tonight?" She glanced at the young man briefly but obviously did not give the question much thought as her gaze resumed searching the crowds.

Then her face brightened when a slender young woman with shoulder-length, brown hair, swinging as she hurried along, emerged from the shadows between the buildings. The late afternoon sun glinted off the red highlights in her hair, and as she approached, her businesslike expression softened into a smile.

"Have you been here long?" she asked the blonde as she approached.

The younger girl, smiling as well, shook her head no.

"Hungry?"

Again there was a negative shake of the curly blonde head.

"Should we go home?"

In response, an odd look flickered across the young blonde's face. It was a look that defies description by an outside observer, but the young woman appeared to understand and just gave the blonde's shoulders a little hug. Using the arm around the narrow shoulders to guide her, she then turned them both to walk toward the bus stop nearby.

As the two waited for the bus, they sat together companionably on the bench, and anyone observing casually wouldn't have noticed anything strange. However, if another person had been sitting there with them, he might have felt a sense of wonderment over how two young women could be so incredibly still for so long. The bus arrived, the two boarded, and the bus disappeared down the street in a cloud of diesel exhaust.

The ride home was just as quiet. Neither young woman seemed in the least uncomfortable nor pressed to say anything at all. Eventually the elder of the two reached up a hand to pull the bell cord to request a stop at the next street, and they rose together and moved toward the exit door. When the bus stopped and the door opened with a *whoosh*, they both hopped down and headed purposefully up the street.

Though they had walked the distance from the bus stop to their Aunt's home fairly quickly, their walk slowed down as they neared the nondescript, ranch-style house nestled into a neighborhood of very similar houses. In fact, the young blonde slowed even more than her sister did until she had fallen well behind. Realizing she was losing her companion, the brown-haired young woman turned with a look of concern in her eyes.

"Bunny," she called softly, her voice compassionate with understanding.

Bunny's large eyes looked up at her for a moment, telegraphing her reluctance, but she did pick up her pace a little, until she had half-way caught up. But then her curly head sank again even lower than before.

After a slight hesitation, Grace gestured for Bunny to follow her, and she led the way around the side of the house and back to the patio. Digging in her back pack, she pulled out a set of keys and, selecting one, unlocked the French doors that opened into what had once been a family room. The room was now furnished with a couple of twin beds, two small desks, and two tall dressers. Grace dropped her books onto one of the desks and said, "Get settled, and I'll go see what I can find for us to eat."

After leaving Bunny alone for about fifteen minutes, Grace returned with a plateful of sandwiches and fruit and a bag of potato chips. She set these offerings down, left again, and returned almost immediately with two strawberry sodas and two yellow paper napkins. Sitting cross-legged on the floor, the two ate together while Grace talked off and on about happenings of the day.

Grace popped a last slice of orange into her mouth before delicately wiping her fingers and mouth with her napkin.

Rising, she said, "Are you done?" When Bunny nodded, Grace stood, stretched, and then gathered up their supper things and carried them off to the kitchen. Returning, she inquired, "Do you have any homework tonight?"

Bunny shook her head.

"Well, then, how about a game of checkers before I start studying?"

Bunny agreed with a quick nod, so Grace went to the closet and pulled out the box, returned to her seat on the floor, and laid out the checkerboard, handing Bunny her playing pieces and arranging her own.

"*This* time I'm going to beat you, kid!" Grace exclaimed.

Bunny just grinned and lined up her playing pieces and then waited for Grace to start.

⊰ | ⊱

When the room finally began to darken and Bunny stood up to turn on a light, Grace looked at her watch. "Oh, I've got to hit the books. Midterms are next week, and I've got a lot to cover before then. Do you have something to read?"

Nodding, Bunny gestured toward the book on the bedside table, a biography of Abraham Lincoln. Grace had noticed that Bunny had recently seemed to develop a lively new interest in American history. At least she had been borrowing and reading a whole series of biographies of famous people who'd been key figures in that history, bringing home a new one as soon as she finished the last.

Grace was glad. She worried about Bunny. For so long she had appeared to grow increasingly sad, showing less and less interest in anything outside her own private thoughts. Moving into junior high had seemed to be almost overwhelming for her. Though she'd never had trouble with schoolwork when she was in elementary school, even if she didn't speak, in seventh grade, with its new kind of challenges, her grades had begun to slip. It was then that the school had arranged for her to meet with a special teacher on a regular basis, someone who could give her the one-on-one attention she needed. For the past two and a half years, Bunny, now in tenth grade, had left school early and gone to her special teacher's house three afternoons a week. Grace didn't know just how the woman did it, but she had gradually made a world of difference.

⊰⊱│⊰⊱

Sometime later she turned to look at her sister and saw that the younger girl had fallen asleep, book in hand, soft blond curls spread across the pillow. Smiling, Grace got up and went over to her, stopping for just a moment to gaze down at her sister. While sleeping she still looked very young and vulnerable, though now relaxed and peaceful. Gently taking the book out of Bunny's hand and laying it on the bedside table, Grace pulled the covers up over Bunny's shoulders, gently tucking them around her, and then bent over and gave her a soft kiss on the forehead. Switching off Bunny's bed lamp, Grace returned to her desk.

Later Grace closed her book and stacked it with her notebook and other texts, ready for morning. She clicked off her light then rose and retrieved her own pajamas, and with a big yawn, she put them on in the moonlight spilling through the window. Then, first making sure the alarm was set for morning, she climbed between the brushed flannel sheets of her own bed with a sigh. At first she curled up on her side to watch her sleeping sister, but soon she rolled to her back and lay for a long time with her open eyes fixed on some invisible point on the ceiling, her mind someplace where only she could go.

The whole house was quiet now, but while the two girls read, their relatives—their mother's half-sister, her husband, and their two children—had been sitting in the living room, watching television and eating popcorn. They'd had no intention of purposely excluding Grace and Bunny. This had just become standard operating procedure for the household. In fact, when the authorities had contacted them after the tragedy, they had been happy to offer the girls a home. They had never been close with the girls' mother or really known the girls as they were growing up, but family is family. Once the girls had arrived, they had bought them any new things they needed, introduced them to their new schools and to some of the other children in the neighborhood. They also made a point to sit and talk with them. In fact, they had done everything they had been able to think of to make the girls feel welcome and to draw them into the household routine, but they never seemed to get through. Even after all these years, the two girls seemed to remain behind their wall of reserve and to avoid the family's company.

The girls' relatives had been offended at first and then just mystified. In the end they simply gave up, continuing to support the sisters materially but allowing them to do as they wished on their own. The two families existed with no actual confrontations, there being little interaction of any kind. After eight years, it was as though the little family of two lived under the same roof but separately, only enclosed by the family of four like a small circle inside a larger circle.

In truth, except for the love they had for each other, Grace and Bunny had cultivated no other close relationships. Bunny was still completely silent. Grace avoided developing close friendships, knowing that any other relationship she had would probably exclude Bunny. Unless they met someone who had enough depth and ability to communicate despite the challenge it presented, the two sisters would remain as they always had been. However, despite their self-imposed isolation, they were growing into educated and beautiful young women.

Grace didn't *feel* like a beautiful young woman though. While other girls her age primped and preened in the mirror for long periods, Grace hardly troubled herself to look into one. She checked her straight, white teeth after brushing, made sure no labels or facings peeked from the necklines of her tops and sweaters, and did little else about looks. With her long, brown hair and its dancing, red highlights; her large, calm, brown eyes; and gentle demeanor, she was incredibly attractive, maybe even more so because she didn't know it.

Bunny, on the other hand, would stare into mirrors for long minutes, though not to adjust her appearance in any way. She would gaze deeply into her own eyes as if asking herself an extremely important and puzzling question. People who knew her had long since stopped asking any but yes or no questions of her. She would shake or nod her head in response but expand her answers no further, whether by gestures, writing, or facial expressions.

Bunny had always remained a good student, completing her school assignments promptly and in a way that demonstrated considerable intelligence. However, the intrusive efforts of elementary school teachers to wring information from her by creating special assignments designed for that purpose had been effectively blocked. Bunny would write highly creative compositions, correct in every way, but reveal nothing personal. She had so frustrated the efforts of some of the staff that her reputation preceded her from one grade to the next until they at last gave up and granted her the privacy she so defended.

Bunny probably wished she were completely invisible, but her short, curly, blonde hair and eyes that were not green, gray, or blue exactly, and her small but increasingly well-proportioned shape drew a lot of attention. She was polite to the girls who approached her, but after experiencing Bunny's deep reserve and her thoughtful and direct gaze with little added response, they usually deemed her impaired and gave up attempts to converse. The boys who attempted to communicate with her, however, received only an expressionless glance. Any persistence on their part would result in Bunny's immediate yet unemotional departure.

Still, the girls' whole life began to change through a conversation with one young man.

2

Greg began to rise but fell to the floor, his feet tangled in the blankets. He kicked free then staggered to his feet and pointed them toward the source of the horrific noise. Stumbling over a shoe, he lurched and fell over a rolling desk chair before stopping himself with an elbow on his desktop. He managed to hit the button of what he considered to be the world's most torturous alarm clock. Still leaning on the desk, Greg composed himself, his blurry thoughts on the necessity of getting another clock.

Nearby church bells chimed a short and cheerful "good morning." That sound brought a warm, comfortable feeling into Greg's heart. He didn't know *why* he liked that particular sound so well. Certainly living so close to the church afforded him easy access to the Saturday youth group, which made Saturday fun and something to look forward to. It was always approved of by parents. The association ran deeper though. There was something solid and strong yet peaceful about those church bells. They reminded him that despite the increasing turmoil of the world around him, there was still a quiet place of refuge to be found.

Heartened, Greg grabbed some clothes and made his way toward the shower. Soon he was a little brighter-eyed with his light brown hair still damp but at least tamed. His lanky, athletic frame clothed in jeans and a T-shirt, Greg strode into the kitchen, smiling at his parents as he sat down at the table, just as his mother laid a full plate at his place.

"Good morning, Mom, Dad. Mom, how do you always know just when I'm going to walk in?"

The gentle-faced woman bustling about, getting pitchers, cups, and more plates on the table, just smiled at him and winked.

The radio on the corner of the counter, usually dusty from disuse, was on this morning, and Greg's dad was staring at it with a fixed expression. As Greg pulled his plate of eggs, sausage, and toast a little closer, the words coming from the radio slowly sank in.

"…terrorist activities are increasing throughout the Middle East, and threats of extreme terrorist measures against any countries aligning themselves with Israel are being made.

"Yesterday in Amman, a US reporter was kidnapped. King Abdullah has issued a statement expressing his deep concern that such an event had occurred in Jordan, saying that Jordanian authorities are vigorously investigating the case. The king also said, however, that they now believe the American was quickly taken out of the country.

"In a further development, two hours ago al-Jazeera television announced that it had received an audio tape from a group claiming responsibility. The name they gave for themselves translates as Holy War of Purification. The group gave the US president one week to formally sever relations with Israel or their captive would be killed.

"When asked by a reporter if there would be any change to the alert level here in the United States, the Secretary of Homeland Defense said no. He went on to say, however, that all citizens should remain alert and that there were continuing concerns about possible terrorist activities here at home.

"Here in Denver, two local men were arrested last night on suspicion of planning to bomb a public building. Few details are available yet, but it is known that they recently bought large quantities of materials that could be made into explosives. Authorities have said only that the matter is under investigation."

As the announcer went on to talk about city and sports news, Greg's thoughts stayed on the international crisis of the day. He found himself fervently thankful that he wasn't the president. He knew other young people who were not just confused by current events but depressed and even afraid for their personal safety. Many had also been troubled by the persistent rumors on the Internet of the draft being revived in the near future.

A quick hug for his mom and a pat on the back for his dad were his silent farewell. He wasn't sure if they were still listening to the now-local news or if their thoughts, like his, had stuck to the international dilemma. In either case, their expressions were rather distracted as they smiled their good-byes, and Greg headed for the door without anything more being said. At least it was a beautiful day outside. The sky was clear and the sun bright, with just a hint of the crispness that told of the changing season. Even now, the leaves on the trees up and down the street were starting to turn. *Of course*, he thought, *that means there will be lots of leaves to rake soon*. But he didn't mind terribly, and he was grinning as he jumped into his twelve-year-old Dodge. Inserting and turning the key, his smile got bigger and he leaned back to listen for just a moment. This weekend he had given his car a major tune-up, and now it purred like a kitten. *Beautiful!* He drove away with a sense of personal satisfaction.

❧ | ☙

School was uneventful until the last five minutes of Greg's last class of the day. There were few particular challenges for him mentally. He had maintained a 3.9 GPA throughout his freshman year without any stress, just good study habits and a self-disciplined social life. Even now that a couple of his courses were proving a little tougher, he had no trouble staying on top of it all.

At the end of his last class of the day, he was just scratching out a few final notes on the lecture, almost ready to make his usual dash out the door to the parking lot to get ahead of the traffic, when a beautiful young woman, a fellow student, walked by his seat. A protruding screw on his desk snagged the sweater she carried over her arm, and as she stopped to free it, he smelled her faint perfume before she turned and continued down the aisle. His head turned to look after her as if it had a will of its own, and before he even realized what he was doing, he had closed his book and followed her out the door and down the hallway.

"Hey," Greg called out when he had almost caught up with her. *That was lame*, he silently berated himself.

"Hey" was about the simplest form of greeting one could come up with. Yet she did stop and turn to look back, a questioning look in her eyes.

"I...I'm sorry about your sweater," Greg stammered, mentally kicking himself again. He was not a shy-boy type. He was also not a player, but he usually had confidence and maturity enough to handle any conversation. For instance, he had recently attended a political rally with his parents. There they had all been introduced to one of Colorado's US senators by a woman his mother knew through her work with the school system. In that case, he'd been able to hold a lively conversation with the senator about current issues. At the end of the conversation, the senator had complimented Greg's astute questions and comments. All this made the feeling he was having at the moment particularly unnerving. He couldn't even tell exactly what the jittery feeling should be attributed to.

"Oh, that's okay," the young woman's voice broke into his frustrated thoughts. "It wasn't your fault; it was your desk's."

"Uh, yes. Well, I apologize for my desk, since it can't speak for itself," Greg replied with his most jaunty smile. *Since it can't speak for itself? Oh no, I'm dead in the water. I apologized for my desk.* His inner man was really pounding on him.

Then she laughed. Oh, what sweet relief that merry sound was! He ventured a peek at her face—prior to her laughter, his eyes had been directed anywhere and everywhere else. Greg was not prepared for the look he encountered. It was the kind of look that completely stops the clock, stops the universe. And it was a look *exchanged* with the girl, not just viewing the girl.

"Could I walk with you?" Greg eventually asked.

"I…I don't know." It was her turn to stammer an answer. She seemed sort of startled then and turned to walk quickly away from him, picking up speed as she headed down the steps and even skipping the bottom step before she headed across campus.

What happened there? Greg asked himself. He knew something delightful had transpired when he had actually looked at her, but then what?

He stood in the same spot for just enough time to end up in the worst traffic jam of the afternoon if he left the campus, so he decided to find a spot to sit for a while and think.

The sun dropped, cherry red, over the horizon, twilight slipping in like a screen saver, while he remained motionless, perched on the stone window ledge in front of the building. He was staring at the ground but was only aware of his inner thoughts about the girl, about the world, and about the girl some more.

Dinner-table conversation was on autopilot for Greg that night. Despite how cordial the atmosphere was, it was relief to be able to excuse himself after helping with the dishes, pleading a need to study. Inside he was a basket case.

What would a serious relationship be like in an unstable setting like the world today, was his next to last challenging thought as his head finally lay back on his pillow that night.

His last challenging thought was, *Can I stand that alarm clock one more morning?*

⌣|⌤

This time the off button seemed easier to find. The sun was behind clouds but still looked brighter to Greg. Breakfast was always good, but this morning's breakfast was great! It seemed to Greg that having to wait all day for his last class was the only problem in his world.

Greg arrived so early for American History that there were only two other people in the big lecture hall. Both were preps with laptops they had to set up for class note taking. Greg watched every person file in and find a seat.

Yesterday's vision arrived precisely on time and glanced quickly around the room before finding a seat near the front. Greg couldn't tell if she had noticed him, but he was filled with a happy and tender feeling as he looked down at the back of her head from his usual spot near the rear door. She seemed vulnerable in some way. Maybe it was how she sat there with her head neither held proudly high nor sullenly low, but steady and quiet, just waiting for information.

Then her shoulders tensed, and she turned her head just a bit, a look on her face as if she were sensing something. Greg felt as though his heart stopped for a second or two as the girl turned in her seat and looked directly at him as if she had discerned that he'd been observing her closely. He sat blinking and returned her look, hoping he didn't appear as dumbfounded as he felt. She gave him a quick smile and turned back around. Greg's soul felt like it had wings and was flying above them all. His normally active mind came to a standstill in a wave of pure happiness.

Then the professor arrived and began to speak, which brought Greg back to the moment, but while he settled into class mode, he began to wonder why one smile from one young woman should make him feel better than all the smiles from all the other girls in his whole young life. He chose not to overanalyze and bring himself down but instead handled this question lightly, bouncing it around in his head while he listened to the professor lecturing about Teddy Roosevelt's unusual personality and contributions.

⇥ | ⇤

"All right, be ready for the midterm tomorrow and have a nice evening."

Class was finally over, and Greg sprang from his seat, dashing out the door and positioning himself at a spot in the hallway where he could monitor the door.

When she emerged from the lecture hall, she also had an expectant look on her face, which pleased him very much and gave him more confidence in his approach. "Hi. I've been waiting to talk with you," he said. "What's your name? Are you ready for the midterm?"

The young woman replied playfully, "Eighteen more and we can play twenty questions." Greg could have been caught off-guard, but although she didn't answer his inquiries, there was something nonthreatening about the way she tossed out that comment. He just chuckled and waited, liking the lack of tension between them. He didn't have to wait long for her to continue.

"I'm Grace Fairchild." She held out her hand. "I'm not quite ready. Are you?"

"I'm Greg Johnson, and I'm ready as I'll ever be," he rejoined, still smiling as he gently took her hand and gave it more of a gentle squeeze than a shake.

Her long eyelashes veiled her eyes, and as nearly as he could tell, she focused on her shoes. He sensed that she was feeling awkward. Surprisingly, she didn't seem practiced in the casual give and take most students tossed around. He knew he would need to carry the conversation if he wanted to get to know her.

"Grace." He said her name gently and thoughtfully. "I like your name. It has a wonderful meaning. Is this your first term here? I'm sure I would have noticed you before now if you'd been here longer." *Smooth, Greg*, he said to himself. Even he thought his last statement sounded like a line.

"Actually, this is my *second* year on campus—"

Greg groaned inwardly, but then he was relieved as her face quickly softened to a shy smile.

"—but thank you for the compliment."

Greg exhaled slowly, realizing that he had been holding his breath. She was not going to be hard on him. Greg's mind raced on. *Then maybe she won't be as hard to talk with as I thought.* "Would you..." he began, but as quickly as it appeared, her smile gave way to a slight frown as she looked at her watch and made a sudden move toward the large double doors leading out of the building.

"I have to meet someone now. I'll see you." Her words trailed off as she headed for the doors.

Greg wasn't ready to let this opportunity end quite so easily and hurried after her, his words rushed. "Let me walk with you a ways, Grace. I was going to offer to help you study for the test if you'd like me to. I mean, you don't know me yet, but I'm a good sort of guy. I'd like a chance for you to find that out for yourself, and I want to get to know you as well. I don't say this sort of thing to just anyone." *Now you're rambling, Greg.* Greg stopped talking and just waited for her reaction.

Grace didn't stop walking, but she didn't turn away either while listening to Greg's little speech. Then she spotted Bunny, who was waiting as usual by the steps of the Administration Building, and Grace stopped suddenly.

"Look," she said seriously, gesturing with a nod, "my sister is waiting right over there. She doesn't speak, and I don't ever like to put her in an awkward situation. I'm afraid I don't know how to handle this."

Yes! thought Greg. *That's not a turndown.* But she surely had given him something to think about and not much time to make a plan. "Uh, why don't you just introduce us and let me give it a try?"

Grace hesitated, looking thoughtfully at his face. Then she gave a barely perceptible nod and led them over to a young woman who looked to Greg like she might be about fifteen or sixteen years old.

3

Rit hated Denver. It wasn't the mountains or the streams or the people. It wasn't the skyline or lack of classic architecture. *It just wasn't Boston.* True, Boston didn't claim to be the cleanest, most elegant, or most crime-free city, but Rit missed his old neighborhood there with its sort of fishy smell and even all the old newspapers rolling in the streets like tumbleweeds. Here there actually were real weeds blowing around the outskirts of Denver in the late summer. And he was having trouble adjusting to the quiet compared to his old neighborhood. The very first day his family had arrived, he had been sitting on the porch for three hours before he realized he had not heard a single gunshot.

He had been called Rit for so long now that he hardly even thought of himself by his given name. Some people he knew kept their Asian names, but many others chose American names, especially at the time they became citizens of the United States. In his case, it wasn't so much a matter of choosing a new name as just having it happen. His new American friends had been fascinated with the fact that, unlike most other Asians they knew, his black hair had distinct reddish highlights. All in good natured fun, one of his new buddies suggested he'd maybe spilled a bit of Rit dye on his head, and they'd quickly dubbed him Rit, and Rit he became to everyone, even his teachers. Only his parents still remembered his birth name, sometimes using it in a moment of stress or when they were being particularly stern with him.

When Rit had found out that they were going to leave Boston and move far away to the west, he'd hated the idea, but he tried to make the best of it by fantasizing about being a pioneer heading out to the Wild West. Once he saw his new home, however, the role was difficult to play out. In reality, Boston was a lot wilder than Denver. In fact, Denver seemed like a hugely overgrown small town to Rit. His analysis was based on the friendly atmosphere and laid-back ways of many people who lived there.

Rit was good at analyzing things. His IQ was near genius level, and he excelled at experimentation, diagnostics, and computer science. Unfortunately, he was also easily bored in a regular classroom. His parents were very aware of the problem, but it had been hard to find a solution back in Boston, first due to the language barrier, which Rit overcame much more quickly than they did, and then because the Boston school Rit had to attend offered little opportunity for the very gifted. The one good thing for Rit in this move, as he saw it, was that the school here was much better than the old one. As soon as his new teachers got an idea of what he could do academically, the school had quickly sent him to the school system's special services coordinator. She had been very nice and had helped him qualify for and then get into some math and science courses at the university, even though he was still only sixteen and a high-school junior.

Some things hadn't changed at all. His mother still chose to cook the way she always had. Rit could count on the same delicious dishes the family had always eaten.

And his father's strict ways and emphasis on a good education remained just as unchanged as their cuisine. He too had been pleased with Rit's new school opportunities and regularly questioned him about his college class work. In fact, those questions could be tough. Rit's grandfather had been part of the Nationalist Chinese military that had retreated to Taiwan when the Communists took over on the mainland. From Taiwan the family had made their way in small groups to America. Most of the family gathered in Boston for their new start. Rit's father, who had already studied law in Taiwan, decided to get an American law degree and found a small college that accepted him and arranged grants and loans to help him meet his goals. After obtaining his degree and passing the bar exam, Mr. Han started a practice to help other immigrants solve legal issues. When he found Rit's needs could not be met where they lived in Boston, Mr. Han relocated to Denver, where he could continue helping immigrants while providing his son with the opportunities he needed for future success.

Despite the good things about their new life, Rit still felt kind of lost. He'd not yet found many friends, and apart from his studies, he found himself at loose ends. Not that the friends he'd left had been good for him. In Boston, without positive challenges in his life, Rit had shown an inclination to devise other contests.

Falling into the wrong circle of friends, boundaries had been pushed and behavior went beyond mischief. Part of his parents' reason for moving had been to get Rit where he might find more satisfactory challenges and a better kind of friends. His father's income was limited, but his parents had found a modest house in Denver that met their needs, and by keeping a careful budget, the family managed to get along.

Rit brought one old friend with him: Ruby. He almost felt like she was a part of him, and he spent a large portion of his free time with her. He admired her looks, took very good care of her, and occasionally even talked to her.

The door behind Rit opened, interrupting his reverie in the afternoon sunshine out on the front porch.

"Come here, please. Get the dishes for me, Rit."

His mother's English was still heavily accented, and sometimes she had to search hard for the right words, but she insisted that they speak English as a family. Rit knew that she and his dad sometimes spoke Mandarin privately, but they believed language immersion was the avenue to fully mastering English, which in turn was essential for progressing in their new lives. They watched a lot of movies and television shows in order to improve their English and to study American ways, as well as to keep up with what was going on in the world. In the same way, his mother had insisted that the whole family practice the use of Western utensils at meals, at least part of the time, so that they would be prepared to socialize politely and confidently with their new countrymen.

Rit was proud of their determination and how much they had accomplished over the past few years. He hadn't meant to get in trouble in Boston. One thing led to another in his peer group, but in his heart he respected his parents, and he would never deliberately cause them grief.

"Yes, ma'am," Rit responded immediately. "Gotta go, Ruby. I'll be back after dinner." He left the brilliant-ruby-colored skateboard on the porch and followed his mother to the kitchen. Helping his mother with dinner made him feel good anyway, as though he were making up for the trouble he had caused them.

As soon as the dining-room table was set and serving dishes were placed on the table, she smiled up at him and patted his hand, the signal that he was excused to go find his father.

Once everyone was seated, the predictable conversation began, even as food was being passed. His father would ask for the details of his classes at school, and then, carefully choosing his English words, he would lecture Rit about the value of education, tying in some current events that illustrated his point. Dinner's conclusion would miraculously coincide with his father's recap, and after politely asking to be excused from the table, Rit would head for the front door.

⇥|⇤

Ruby had adventurous wheels. She and Rit rolled to a new part of the city each time they went out together, which was every day, at least once, rain or shine.

Rit was fascinated by the fact that each part of the city had its own smell. Downtown smelled like hot, slightly rancid grease, doughnuts, and bus exhaust. The very poor part of town smelled like garbage, the odor of stale beer wafting out of run-down bars, and odd little clouds of cheap perfume scattering at random as people milled around. The part of the city where a lot of Asian people had settled smelled like familiar foods cooking and different types of incense coming from shops and homes along the way.

The curious wheels carried Rit another direction this evening. As he rolled along, he noticed the aroma of freshly cut grass and brilliant displays of autumn flowers all neatly laid out. The homes were getting larger and the driveways longer as he went. There was also a woodsy smell in the air that drew him on. Coming around a curve in the street, he found a small park filled with spruce and reddening maples, and with a quick movement of his foot, he popped Ruby into the air, caught her in his hand, and continued on foot up the drive and into the trees.

Now, this definitely isn't like Boston, Rit thought to himself, but he liked it. He liked the spongy way the grass responded under his feet. He loved how the sun cast dramatically interlocking shadows all around him. He dropped his skateboard onto the ground and then seated himself on it, propping his arms on his knees and relaxing as he looked around him, taking in the stillness. Only a playful squirrel and the raucous call of a crow ruffled the calm.

He sat there in the middle of a patch of remaining sunlight until it faded away.

⊰ǁ⊱

Rolling home was dreamlike in the half dark. This was Rit's favorite time of day. He was a night person, but he managed to function within the constraints of a society that strongly preferred a day schedule. He still got his best ideas though and did his most efficient work later in the evening. Tonight he intended to finish an especially challenging computer assignment for one of his professors when he got home.

Rit was crossing the last street in this new territory when a dark-colored Mercedes rolled around the corner.

4

Brian disliked the new Mercedes but didn't want to snub his father's gift. **He** really thought the car fairly shouted, "Look at me! I have everything you've ever wanted." He kept his thoughts to himself, though; he loved his parents and didn't want to hurt them. Besides, it wasn't just this car; it was their whole lifestyle…

"Thank you very much, sir," was what came out of his mouth.

"You're very welcome, son," replied the distinguished-looking older man. "We're proud of your success."

"Will you and Mother make it to the debate?" asked Brian.

"I'm sorry. I have to be back in Washington, Brian, and I don't know your mother's itinerary yet. She's supposed to e-mail that to me before my four o'clock flight this afternoon." Even as he answered, the senator strode over to an almost identical but older model Mercedes parked on the other side of the drive. "Even if we're not in attendance, we always wish you the best, son. You know that." He bent down and sort of folded his six feet five inches into his car, started it, put it in gear, and then drove away without delay, all in one smooth process.

Brian wondered if he would ever reach his father's height. Now twenty, he suspected he'd finished his growth, but at six three, he still towered above many other young men on campus.

Brian let his brain spin onto more pleasant things, away from anything that could get him down. *After all,* he'd told himself, *many people have hard things to deal with in their lives. My problems are very minor when you think about all the real misery suffered by millions of people in the world.*

Brian did his best to keep everything light, at least on the face of it, although he actually felt things very deeply. He followed current events closely, and he had a particular interest in the serious challenges facing many people, even in this country. What was more, he had a gift for seeing things from others' points of view, a gift refined through his frequent conversations with the many kinds of people he ran into in the course of his days—everyone from the university's dean of students to a homeless man downtown. He asked lots of questions and did lots of listening. In a way, his search for truth was what led him to choose political science for a major. He didn't want just to copy his father's career, but he did look for ways that he could make a difference.

He caught a glimpse of some lint on the sleeve of his lightweight, blue sweater and picked it off meticulously. Then, with a deep sigh, he turned and cut between the grand old trees of the arboretum, past the formal garden that graced the front lawn of the large, native-stone mansion, and entered the house through its heavily carved oak door. Even with the door closed behind him, the scent of mums and the last of the roses lingered in his olfactory memory as he crossed the large marble-floored foyer and trotted up the wide grand staircase to the second floor.

His suite of rooms was at the far end of the west wing, the opposite end of the house from his parents' suites. On the first floor beneath him were guest rooms and the library—Brian's favorite spot apart from his own rooms. Central on the ground level, opening into the large foyer, was the ballroom. On the nights when his parents gave one of their big holiday-time parties, he could hear the music and laughter, but the rest of the time it was very quiet in his rooms.

Once upstairs, Brian wasted no time in changing shoes and retrieving his golf clubs from the closet in the entry to his suite. He'd already put them away for the season, but on such an inviting morning, he couldn't resist getting them out again.

He chose the quicker way downstairs offered by the servants' stairs in back. This brought him down to the back hallway, right next to the kitchen. He seldom went in the kitchen—the cook could be fierce when anyone invaded her workspace—but his favorite apples had been missing from the fruit basket upstairs, and he wanted to see if there were more in the cooler.

His venture successful and with apple in hand, he headed out the back door and toward the garage before he remembered that he had a new car parked in front. As he walked around the house, Brian admonished himself silently not to allow the reluctance about accepting the new car to interfere with his use of it. *Lots of guys would be delighted to have that car,* he told himself, and he pushed back the nagging feeling of shame he got at the thought of driving it around. Still, there were hungry people in the world. He knew some of them and contributed to the food pantries and soup kitchens in the city. He believed in personal moderation. His choosing the State University when he would have been accepted just about anywhere solidly represented his views. His parents' lifestyle did not reflect the same values he held.

Brian thought of the family history portraits that graced the upstairs central hall. Some were old photographs or sketches, others professionally painted portraits, all now beautifully framed. One stuck out, startling when set in the line of serious, dark-skinned faces. All together, the portraits told quite a story.

It all started with a conscience-stricken slave owner in antebellum Georgia—a man who had owned Brian's great-great-great-grandparents. John Sommers, a South Carolina plantation owner, had inherited his big place near the coast from his father and never thought too much about the right or wrong of it. But even as he prospered over the years, he watched the tightening of slaves' bondage and finally found it intolerable.

One day a relative in the north sent him some clippings from abolitionist publications. John read them, and though his neighbors angrily dismissed them, he couldn't quite forget their message.

Then he made a trip to New York on business. While he was there, a friend took him to hear a speech by the former slave Frederick Douglass. John was very impressed. When he got home, he was even more disturbed when he looked around with his newfound enlightenment. At last he decided he had to do something to right the wrong being done, at least in his little corner of the world.

The laws at that time didn't allow him to educate his slaves, but he did start doing all the simpler things he could to better their lives. He quit buying and selling people. A harsh overseer was fired, families were identified and moved into cabins together, and he started personally making sure everyone had better food and clothing and adequate time for rest and recreation. He caught more than a little criticism from neighbors, but he also noticed that his already profitable plantation became even more profitable, as well as becoming a happier place.

He also started quietly working out how all his slaves could finally gain their freedom. He shocked his distant relatives and community when he suddenly sold the plantation outright, including most of its furnishings, and freed every man, woman, and child. In addition, he gave each family or single person enough money for a good start in a new life. He even arranged transportation north for all who wished to go. He then packed up his personal possessions and moved to Connecticut, where at least he would not have to watch firsthand the bitter destruction war would bring to the South.

Brian's ancestors, Julius and Sophie, were among the many former Sommers slaves who gladly adopted the family name of the former plantation owner. This black Sommers family moved to Boston. Julius then put his old blacksmith and wagon-mending skills to work, soon developing a nice business. Sophie became a seamstress.

Seeing that their children were educated was just as important to the Sommers as making a living. They found someone to teach their oldest son, and as he learned, Sophie asked him to teach her too, so she could read her Bible and keep better business records. They both taught the younger children.

And from their first day of freedom, they lived frugally and planned carefully how to grow their money, teaching their children to do the same. Their joy was complete when they saw their grandsons go to college and three of that generation establish professions.

It was Brian's grandfather, a doctor, who turned out to have a particular gift for successful money management. Coming to Denver to hang out his shingle, he had seen opportunity in the growing city. Ignoring the stock market, which he knew could be fickle, he began investing in real estate outside city limits, where he knew the city and its suburbs would eventually grow. As his accurate foresight began to pay off handsomely, he gradually broadened into commercial real estate and new business start-ups. By the time he died, he was a multimillionaire, though he had never abandoned his integrity or the commitment to avoiding waste or had given in to pointless extravagance.

Charles Sommers, Brian's father, owed many of his opportunities in life to this family history. Even his successful political career had been made possible by the wealth and connections it provided. A portrait of old John Sommers hung in a place of honor in the family gallery upstairs. Sometimes Brian would pause before it, wondering what the old gent with tufts of white hair sticking up like dandelions going to seed and wildly curling eyebrows over laughing gray eyes would think of all that his nonconformist actions had set in motion.

As for him, Brian knew he looked incredibly similar to his own Grandfather Sommers, whose portrait hung in the same hallway. Brian had the same refined, dark features, the same intelligent light shining in his eyes, and the same set jaw. People said their personalities were even quite similar. Brian was aware of the likeness due to other people's constant mention, but not dwelling on his own attributes, he usually just acknowledged the comments with a vague smile and a brief nod.

⊰꙰ | ꙰⊱

The trunk of his new Mercedes was a pleasant surprise. It had ample space for golf clubs and other sports gear. Brian excelled at most sports he had tried, and he could easily have tried going pro in golf if he hadn't set his eyes on public service. But golf well played still provided him a happy recreational outlet, and he willed his body and mind to relax as he drove to the club. When he had to stop for a red light, he leaned over to check out the back seat, and there it was, as he expected. His dad had had a mini bar put in, just like his own. Brian opened it and found it was even stocked. Extracting a cold Perrier, he opened it and drank as he drove on without taking his eyes off the road.

He shook his head, bemused by the conflicting ideals bumping around inside it. He loved his parents and truly enjoyed the wonderful gifts they had bestowed on him since birth. He wanted to display his gratitude, but it was weighted with the sinkers of humanitarian ideals that whispered questions and opened his eyes to other people's deprivation. He let the cool water assuage the dryness in his throat, wishing there was something that would treat his mind likewise.

⚜ | ⚜

The drive home was tempered by exercise and fresh air. Brian definitely felt better after eighteen holes and a tall glass of herbal iced tea. He stopped at the local flower shop and chose a "welcome home" bouquet for his mother. By now this was a tradition.

His father was in Washington most of the time when Congress was in session. During recesses or any weekends when he came home to cultivate his constituency, he often seemed to be just as occupied; his schedule was a busy round of political events and trips out of town for speaking engagements. When he was in Denver, he always tried to touch base with Brian, but planned times together often had to be postponed or cancelled, and now that Brian's own schedule was busier, the two men seemed to see less and less of each other.

Brian's mother also traveled a lot, dividing her time between Washington, political activities in Colorado, and trips around the country on behalf of the various charitable organizations and foundations she worked with. She'd always been busy, but once Brian reached his later teens, his parents felt free to leave him home by himself, and she was gone even more frequently and for longer periods. He had started leaving flowers on the table for his mother whenever she was due to return home, just to make her aware that he was attentive to her schedule, that he cared about her comings and goings. For her part, she was not a cold or unfeeling person, and she did love her son, but it was hard for Brian to tell just what the flowers said to her. She genuinely delighted in receiving them, but she didn't seem to perceive the soul of her son reaching out to her. Mrs. Sommers wore activity like a whirlwind mantle, and it seemed that not many things of a personal nature got her attention.

Brian's attention was caught when the car radio switched from music to a news broadcast. As he listened to the latest on events in the Middle East, he frowned. In the face of terrorism, which Brian considered a result of illiterate, hungry, and jealous men converted into helplessly raging religious fanatics, he felt inadequate. Scrutinizing his own morals first and then applying the evaluation nationwide, he discovered enough selfishness and pride to be able to see how jealousy and hatred might be kindled in any disadvantaged country. He suspected that their own greed for power was what motivated men like Osama bin Laden and Abu Musab al-Zarqawi to incite their compatriots to such violence, so often in the name of religion. Unmasking the bad guys and educating entire nations so that they would no longer be so easily manipulated was a task worthy of the best politicians and professors. Getting the home players to stay on the same page was another kind of challenge. *Maybe if they could just find a similar page…*

Brian's thoughts started to zero in on specifics. Ever the political analyst, he looked at key aspects of world problems like a gem expert magnifies a many-faceted gem under special lighting, turning it endlessly to examine it from minutely different angles.

Brian's mind was thus occupied when he turned the corner near his home. Noticing a dark shape ahead in the twilight, he quickly veered to the left but not quickly enough. He heard a loud *crack,* and his heart leaped into his throat.

⊰ | ⊱

If he hadn't jumped off Ruby and thrown himself to the side, ending up half in and half out of the street, he might have ended up like the skateboard. The driver of the car, hearing the terrific *crack*, pulled over immediately. A tall, attractive, young black man, only a few years older than Rit, dressed in Dockers and a blue sweater, appeared and quickly approached Rit. He held half a skateboard in his hand and had a very concerned look on his face.

Rit was lying awkwardly on his back, sort of upside down, with his head off the curb and his feet up the grassy slope into someone's yard. The other young man reached out his hand to pull Rit to his feet. Rit muttered his thanks but didn't even want to look at Ruby, a fact the other guy seemed to notice.

"I'm so sorry about your skateboard. Are you all right? I didn't see you at all! Why don't you wear reflectors or something? Are you hurt?"

"No," Rit responded, answering the last question first. "I'm not hurt. I didn't know I would be out this late." His voice trailed off sadly, and a long silence ensued.

❖ | ❖

The driver of the Mercedes was trying to decide how much responsibility he had. He hadn't broken any laws, so the question of legal liability was under control. It was the ethical question that was giving him trouble at the moment. "Look, I would feel better if you'd let me take you home. Brian Sommers is my name. What's yours?" The young man held out his hand again.

❖ | ❖

Rit hesitated slightly before he shook the outstretched hand. He didn't mean to feel resentful. He knew it wasn't the young man's fault, but the loss of Ruby was already painful. His skateboard was the thread that kept his private life together. "I'm Rit," he finally replied. He looked the other young man right in the eye but disclosed nothing of his own feelings. "I would appreciate a ride home." He was put out, but he wasn't stupid. A ride home would definitely bring this disastrous evening to a quicker close, with less chance of repercussions for being late.

"Great! Hop in. Where am I going?" said Brian without further ado.

"Is it okay if I just tell you as we go?" asked Rit as he slowly got into the front seat, gazing at the dashboard, which displayed every imaginable gauge.

Brian put the two halves of the skateboard into the trunk. "Sure," he agreed as he got in, turning the car in the direction Rit had been heading.

The lit-up controls cast an eerie light on the two, their silence broken only by Rit's infrequent directions.

By the time they rolled up to the modest one-and-a-half-story house where Rit's parents sat on the porch waiting, it was dark and the outside temperature was very cool. When the car pulled up, the two older people just observed motionlessly, but when Brian took the broken board out and handed it to Rit, Rit's mother stood up quickly, dropping her shawl onto the rough boards of the porch. His father also stood but more slowly, picking up his wife's shawl as he straightened up. They waited there as Rit and Brian spoke briefly in low tones, Rit eventually turning to walk toward them as Brian drove away into the night. They waited quietly when Rit paused at the bottom of the porch steps with his head lowered before he raised his eyes to look at them and moved forward, taking one gloomy step at a time. His father exchanged a look with his mother over the top of Rit's head and then put his arm around his son's shoulders. He handed his wife her shawl as he and Rit went into the house.

The house was very still that evening. Rit sat in his bedroom working on the computer project he had happily anticipated earlier, but now even that had a sad flavor. He wished he could invent a time machine and go back an hour or two. *If I could,* he thought, *I would wait just another minute before crossing that road and…*

⊹≒|≓⊹

A sense of incompleteness followed Brian as he drove away. He liked this kid and didn't know exactly why. Rit hadn't given him much to go on. Before Brian got home, he decided what he was going to do.

5

"Greg, this is my sister, Bunny. Bunny, meet Greg from my history class," Grace said, a little breathlessly.

Bunny didn't smile, only giving her sister a quizzical glance.

Oh, maybe this wasn't such a good idea, Grace thought. *Maybe I shouldn't have…*

Greg's greeting was perfectly unruffled, however. "Hi, Bunny. Cool name. I talked your sister into letting me hang out."

Bunny looked Greg directly in the eye for a moment, apparently sizing him up. His gaze met hers comfortably. Then Bunny turned back toward Grace with a tiny grin creeping across her lips.

Grace was taken aback by the look she immediately interpreted as, *You kind of like this guy, don't you?* She decided to punt and turned back to Greg. "We take the bus home. Would you like to walk to the bus stop with us?"

"Absolutely," Greg responded, and they set off down the uneven sidewalk.

As they walked, Bunny's toe caught a corner of the pavement that was sticking up, her stumble causing her sweater to slip off her shoulders. Greg noticed and caught it before it touched the ground. He gently returned the sweater to her shoulders with a little pat and a smile, Bunny reciprocating with a grateful expression.

Grace, who was nervously watching both, trying to read every innuendo, had a sudden sense of well-being. Used to feeling the weight of the whole world, this unburdened feeling caught her totally by surprise. She almost wanted to stop and just experience it. She actually did pause for a moment, one foot on the curb, and closed her eyes so briefly the others didn't even notice, before walking on toward the bus stop, now with a lingering tranquility.

True to his word, Greg struck up a chatty conversation with Grace, careful to include Bunny with eye contact and his famous boyish grin. He directed rhetorical questions toward Bunny and specific queries at Grace. His approach was such a success that no one even noticed the huge bus until it pulled up with a snort and screeching brakes right in front of them.

"Uh, I need to run an errand or two before we go home," Grace faltered, startled by the noisy advent of the bus.

"Hey, I've got a great idea then! How 'bout if I get you girls some burgers. We can talk about that homework a bit if you're not going straight home and if Bunny wouldn't get too bored with history."

Grace looked at Bunny, who raised her eyebrows very high and cheerfully shook her head no to being bored. *Today seems to be the day for making quick decisions*, Grace thought, but said aloud, "Well…okay," with only a little hesitation.

They hurriedly got on the bus, and responding to the bus driver's irritated look, Greg apologized, saying,

"Sorry for the delay, sir. You got another passenger out of it, though."

The driver rolled his eyes upward and put the bus in gear with a roar and puff of smoke.

The threesome agreed to eat first, shop later, and as the bus moved along, the hamburger idea evolved to Chinese food. Their destination was a small strip mall fairly close to the university that had both a Chinese restaurant and a large department store.

The trio was seated in a tiny room with only four tables and a lot of atmosphere. Leaving Greg at the table to order hot tea, the two girls excused themselves to wash their hands. As they used the blower to dry their hands, Bunny suddenly threw her arms around Grace in a spontaneous hug. Grace sensed that Bunny was joyfully anticipating dinner. Grace's remaining fears about the situation evaporated like the water on her hands.

When they returned to the table, Grace was determined to find a way to incorporate their nonverbal communication into a cohesive discussion. She began her efforts by pointing out some of Bunny's preferences on the menu, as Bunny joined in with affirmative indications. Greg's enjoyment of the process showed clearly on his face. If he had known their history, he would have felt a wonderful sense of satisfaction. Grace was viewing Bunny's breakthrough with a deepening appreciation for the young man who facilitated it, even though he didn't realize his impact.

Dinner was delicious—the best the girls had ever eaten. Grace enjoyed herself more than she had at any time that she could remember, and even Bunny, who had been so unapproachable in social settings, appeared truly relaxed and delighted. Grace and Greg went over the test material, after which he picked up the check, and the three locked arms like old friends as they headed to the department store nearby.

Grace was surprised that it had gotten dark while they dined, and just as they reached the store entrance, she glanced at her watch.

"Curfew?" Greg asked.

Grace had never applied the concept to herself and her sister before. "Curfew? Oh no, we don't have one."

A flicker of surprise flashed across Greg's face, but he didn't press the matter. He simply gave Grace a grave smile and held the door open for the girls to enter the store.

Bunny pointed out silly knickknacks as the little group wandered around in the big store and made funny faces in response to people, things, and situations. Indeed, her features were so expressive that it was as though she were talking volumes, just like any teenager enjoying getting to know a new friend.

He doesn't realize how special this is, Grace thought, *or that Bunny is purposely making this all work so well, rather than keeping to herself like she usually does*. Grace, however, understood this, and seeing her sister reaching out in this unaccustomed way made her love her more than ever.

For his part, Greg was relaxed and laughing along with Bunny's spirited clowning. And every so often, he paused in the cheerful banter going on to take another look at the beautiful young woman beside him, a touch of wonder in his eyes.

Through the store they went, picking up the items the girls had come for and finally ending up by the back wall, which was lined with bikes, scooters, and skateboards. It was an awesome sight, a huge display with many styles in each section and every color imaginable. Another shopper, a well-dressed young black man, already stood before the skateboard display, posed in deep thought, as Greg, Grace, and Bunny came down the aisle.

He acknowledged them with a bewildered expression. "Every color in the rainbow and none ruby red!"

They looked from the man to the wall of skateboards and saw that although there were several shades of red, none had a ruby-red finish. Each one of the three faces registered an empathetic look all its own as they turned back to him. The sight was so funny and endearing that the tall young man gave a little chuckle and a short explanation to the group regarding the reasons for his search.

They captured the essence of his need, and Greg was the first to offer a solution, "I know! There's a small sports store about half a block away from here. Their inventory isn't as large, but they probably have a different selection. I forget the name of the place, but it's the only other one I know of in this part of town."

"Great! Thanks! Please, what are your names?" The stranger inquired politely. Greg introduced himself, and Grace offered her own and Bunny's names. "Brian

Sommers," he presented himself, shaking Greg's hand. "Grace, Bunny," he said to the sisters, nodding. "Pleased to meet you. Guess I'd better be going before the store closes. Thanks again, Greg." With a wave of his hand, he was gone.

"Wouldn't you hate to hit somebody with your car?" Grace remarked.

"I would hate to hit somebody with a *bicycle*," Greg responded, going one better.

Bunny wiggled her fingers in the air to get their attention then pointed with a mischievous look toward a unicycle leaning on a rack.

"Right," said Greg, laughing as he pulled it toward him and tried to get on. "Even a unicycle could do some damage if a person could actually get on it and ride it." He made several attempts to do just that, but failing every time, he only succeeded in making them break up in laughter, Bunny's silent smiles just as wholehearted as Grace's. When he finally managed to get the tire stuck between two barrels, sending him sprawling over the tops, Greg gave up. With mock dignity he dusted off his clothes and offered an arm to each of his companions. Posturing great sophistication, they made their purchases and exited, noses in the air, eyes twinkling merrily.

Greg walked Grace and Bunny to the bus stop and waited with them. Grace barely had time to thank him for dinner, coaching her for the test, and the wonderful company he had provided before the bus arrived.

Seated on the bus, looking out the window, Bunny silently laughed again, her upper body vibrating with mirth. Grace followed her look as the bus pulled away from the curb and saw Greg quickly heading away from them down the street to catch a different bus to go back to campus and collect his car. At this distance he was identifiable mostly by the outline of his now extremely unruly hair, which stood out in every direction. She smiled a gentle smile and turned to find Bunny's amused eyes about two inches from her own. She stared a bit and then leaned her forehead lightly on Bunny's for a second. She opted for understatement. "Fun day," she said as they settled in their seats for the ride home.

⊰❘❱

After putting his car in the garage, Brian stood in the darkness behind his house and just breathed the crisp air, listening to the faint bark of a dog, the far away hum of a car motor, then the deep silence. He eventually went indoors, automatically keying in the security code and turning up the house lights. Walking through the house to the foyer, he placed his mother's flowers on the antique table near the front door, turning the card so that she could easily see what it said. "Welcome home, Mother! Missed you much. Love, Brian," was today's variation on the theme of their relationship. He had always missed having a mother.

⊰❘❱

Rit had dropped his chin down on his crossed arms, which rested on the desktop. His musings turned into the hypnagogic imagery that marks the state between wakefulness and sleep, and then into short dreams, and finally a long involved dream. He was running through the woods looking everywhere for a treasure. He didn't know what the treasure was, but he was looking under bushes and inside fallen trees. A girl with curly, golden hair appeared in a spot of sunlight and seemed to merge with the light itself. He wanted to ask her if she had discovered the treasure, but every time he moved toward her, she moved away, even though she hadn't appeared to notice that he was there. She moved from light to shadow, and he followed until he became a little afraid he was lost in the forest. The girl glided into a shadow and faded from his view, and he, trying to catch up, tripped over a branch lying on the ground, falling, falling…

Rit awoke abruptly in the half dark. For a moment he didn't realize that he had fallen out of his chair onto the floor. Taking a sleepy peek with one eye at the illuminated numbers on his clock, he decided just to climb back onto his chair and continue working on his computer. He became totally immersed again in the program until he heard a car's horn honk lightly outside his house.

He refocused on the world around him, realizing the smell of cooking was wafting up the stairs into his room and shy sunlight had begun to look in the window. He moved the curtains, looking down with amazement at the street below. The Mercedes from the evening before was parked in front of the house, the driver waving merrily and smiling up at him.

6

Rit gave his window a little tap in the lower right corner before lifting it up. It usually stuck. He leaned out a way, cupping his hand around his mouth. "I'll be right down," he called. Brian gave an affirmative nod as Rit's head disappeared back inside the house.

Thumping down the stairs, pausing only to tell his mother he would be back in for breakfast soon, Rit headed out the door. He hesitated right outside. Usually he grabbed Ruby and ramped off the porch onto the walkway, but he caught himself and did not look at the place Ruby had occupied. Going forward on foot, he greeted Brian with solemn question marks in his eyes.

"Good morning!" Brian said cheerfully.

Rit's expression in response to Brian's good cheer betrayed a certain grumpiness, maybe even a remaining sense of irritation toward Brian, but then he changed it to something more polite. "Hey, what's up?"

"I've got something to show you!" Brian's excitement was even more evident as he popped the car trunk and bounded around to open it wide, motioning for Rit to look inside. Rit peered inside the trunk and then backed away slightly, casting a shocked look at Brian. Brian didn't know how to read that expression, so he waited. As he waited, Rit's eyes returned to the object in the trunk, and he just stared. Finally Brian broke the silence. "Is it okay?"

"Is it for me?" Rit's excitement in spite of himself showed in the appearance of a slight accent.

Brian's sensitive ear caught the feeling behind the words, and he smiled with relief. The gift could have been rejected for many reasons. "Yes, it's for you," he said and leaned against his car, folding his arms with satisfaction.

Rit carefully took the ruby-red skateboard out of the trunk and examined it, stroking the smooth, glossy finish and turning it over to check out the wheels. "Thanks, man," he said softly. "It's a good one!" Then, pausing only slightly, he turned to Brian. "You hungry?"

The kid is full of surprises, Brian thought as he contemplated the breakfast invitation. Even though it wasn't his habit to drop in on families at mealtime, he had a feeling that he should accept the offer. "You offering me breakfast?"

A grin popped out on Rit's face as quickly as the sun comes out from behind a cloud on a windy day, and he turned, gesturing for Brian to follow him into the house. It was the first smile Brian had seen on that young face during their brief acquaintance, and the sight of it brought that sense of relief and closure Brian had been seeking.

More at ease, he followed his young host into the house to meet Rit's parents, who were both in the kitchen. Rit's father, erect and dignified, was sitting at the table, a newspaper unfolded beside him. Rit's mother, petite and with a porcelain-doll delicacy to her looks, was just setting the table as they walked in, her quiet energy and firm step belying her delicate appearance.

Brian took in the atmosphere in the small kitchen. These weren't just quiet people, he decided. They had a deep stillness about them. Noting that they seemed to be undisturbed by his unexpected appearance presented a puzzle for Brian. *On one hand, they would probably make a stranger welcome—even at breakfast. On the other hand, if it was the stranger that managed to threaten their usually tranquil lives by almost running over their son—* Brian looked around for evidence of more siblings and saw none—*maybe their only son, they might not be so welcoming.*

Rit had carried the skateboard in with him, something he never did. This unusual event got his parents' attention, and they accurately sized the situation up, both smiling up at Brian in perfect harmony.

Drama over, Brian said to himself as Rit's mother spoke. "Please sit down with your friend, Rit. We are almost ready here."

Rit's dad spoke more formally. "Welcome to our home Mr...."

He paused slightly while Rit supplied Brian's name. "Sommers."

He then continued, extending his hand. "Han Shou Ling and my wife, Woo Jen."

"Pleased to meet you, Mr. and Mrs. Han," Brian responded, shaking hands with both of them.

"Please have a seat, Mr. Sommers." With a gesture and a smile, Mrs. Han invited him to be seated at the place she had just set next to Rit.

"Please call me Brian, if you would," Brian said, taking the seat offered.

Mrs. Han then placed steaming dishes before them and took her own seat, joining them for what turned out to be a wonderful meal. It was unique for Brian, since he'd never had noodles for breakfast before, but they were good, and he very much enjoyed the interesting company.

As everyone ate, Rit's parents drew Brian as well as their son into a lively conversation, much of it about current events—very current. It turned out that Mr. Han rose early every morning and watched the news as he drank a cup of hot tea. The older gentleman was very interested when he discovered who Brian's father was and asked some very well-informed questions about the issues in the upcoming elections. As usual, Brian was quite prepared to delve into such matters thoughtfully, though he restrained himself from asking personal questions for fear of giving offense.

Finally, as she began clearing the table, Brian thanked Rit's mother with sincere compliments. Then, realizing the time, he quickly excused himself, not wanting to make Rit late for school. He ended up wishing, though, that there was more time to spend with this family. He found Mr. Han a fascinating man. He was obviously well educated as well as friendly and caring in the way he related to this young stranger who had shown up unexpectedly, despite his formal manner. Brian would have loved to find out more about his background and just how the family came to be in the United States, not to mention Denver. He had noticed the deepened lines in Mr. Han's face, making him look older than he probably was, and Brian suspected there was quite a story to be told.

⚜ | ⚜

Rit rushed to get ready for school—showering, dressing, throwing his backpack over one shoulder, dashing downstairs and out the door—stopping only long enough to pick up his new skateboard and tell his parents good-bye and when to expect him home. Outside, he hopped on Ruby II, so he'd conditionally christened her, and kicked himself into motion. Soon he was far down the street.

As he approached the nearest major street, he glanced at the big diver's watch on his wrist. *Not too bad. I'll make it on time*, he was thinking as he looked up again—just in time to avoid running into the cutest blonde, curly haired girl he'd ever seen. *Wow! Wish I could have stopped to check that out*, his thoughts bubbled. *Get run over, run over somebody. I should learn to pay attention.*

⚜ | ⚜

For her part, the girl just cast him a look that said quite clearly, *Learn how to drive!* and walked on. Then she turned back for a second look, a slightly puzzled expression on her face. But it was not the boy himself as much as the skateboard that she was checking out. She then walked on, but thoughtfully. Soon, however, she reached her destination, the home of the school system's special services coordinator.

When the school had referred Bunny to her a couple of years earlier, it was expected that Bunny would be directed to other service providers. Instead, Mrs. Johnson had felt particularly drawn to this silent young lady and decided to take Bunny under her own wing. Normally Bunny came over three afternoons a week, but because she had conflicts with their next couple of regular sessions, Mrs. Johnson had arranged with the school for Bunny to come early today and spend the whole school day.

As Bunny came up the steps of the old but well-kept Victorian house, her teacher met her at the door, inviting her in with a warm smile that deepened the smile lines around her eyes—the only obvious wrinkles in her face, which was still youthful.

"I thought we might start this day with milk and some coffeecake that I just baked before we get down to work. Sound good to you?"

Bunny smiled her agreement and followed Mrs. Johnson to the sunny kitchen at the rear of the house. By the time she'd enjoyed a morning visit with her tutor—comfortable even though silent on one side—and then become involved with her studies, Bunny had all but forgotten about the handsome, red-haired boy on the red skateboard.

⇥|⇤

The boy did not forget about Bunny, though. Throughout the day, Rit experienced a nagging feeling that he'd met her before or knew her from some other place. He placed her in one past situation after another in his mind, but none fit. When he tried to dismiss the puzzle entirely, it just floated back at inopportune moments, like when he caught a glimpse of a blonde-haired girl leaving the cafeteria at lunchtime and the cashier had to repeat his total three times before he collected his thoughts and paid her. In Computer Science class, the professor used Rit's program for an example without his even realizing it. The teacher had shown it, explained it, and twice asked Rit for acknowledgment before Rit, hearing his name, surfaced from his curly-blonde dilemma to find the whole class looking at him expectantly and the instructor impatiently tapping a pencil on the overhead projection screen. The class time was actually up, and, pulling it together quickly, he made a joke about working the program out in his dreams while he slept at his desk. The class laughed, the instructor grimaced, and everyone piled out of the classroom.

As Rit emerged from the building, he caught himself looking around for the girl. Instead of finding her, he found himself looking straight into Brian Sommers's amazed eyes.

"You go here?"

"Yes, I take some courses here to keep me busy and out of trouble," Rit replied.

"So, is it working?" Brian asked, his smile softening the question.

Rit laughed. "I have all I can handle, man. How 'bout you?"

"Junior year. I need a couple math courses, one required for my major. Put it off as long as I could."

Rit picked up on the sarcasm. "You have trouble with numbers?"

"Not when they're referencing the polls." Brian unconsciously squared his shoulders as he spoke, and Rit could tell Brain was uncomfortable with revealing his weakness with mathematics, but what he said next showed a remarkable ability to subjugate pride. "Actually, math is my worst subject, which is why I put it off. Brilliant decision! Now I have calculus *and* statistics, not to mention physics, which also has a bear of a lab."

"Can I see which books you have?" Rit propped his skateboard up against the retaining wall next to them.

"Um, sure." Brian unsnapped his leather briefcase and pulled out the three large volumes inside, handing them over.

"Uh huh," Rit commented, handing them back.

"Uh huh, *what*?"

"I've already taken all three of these classes," Rit stated flatly. "Exactly the same. Summer term."

"How did you do?" Brian's tone let Rit know that Brian already kind of knew the answer.

"I got A's," was his simple reply with absolutely no offending arrogance. Brian nodded his head thoughtfully, looking down at the sidewalk and just waited. Then the offer came.

"I could help you get a good grade too. It's a breeze if you look at them the right way."

Brian stooped down to situate the books in his briefcase and appeared to be mulling over Rit's offer as he did so. When he stood up again, he carefully responded. "I know you didn't make this offer for money, and you may not need any. You seem very intelligent, and you'll probably be getting scholarships and awards," he paused and Rit waited patiently while Brian searched for words, "I would feel so much better, though, if you would let me pay you for tutoring me."

Rit felt pretty sure that it was his dignity that Brian was being so careful of, and he appreciated his sensitivity, but his own mind quickly evaluated the situation a different way. He didn't have a job, didn't have time to work around his studies, and knew the family could always use more income. He could tutor, enjoy pursuing a possible new friendship, *and* study his own subjects all at the same time—an efficient solution to his time management challenges! In less than the blink of an eye, he answered, "Okay."

"Okay?" Rit detected a note of respect and curiosity in Brian's voice.

"Yep."

"Unfortunately, my midterms in all of the above begin Friday—just two days from now. So maybe we could start fresh next week?" Brian suggested.

But Rit had a plan of his own. His culture was not one that procrastinated on academic endeavors. He also had all the humble confidence necessary to carry out his counter offer and had strategically, evaluated Brian's potential. "If we get right on this, you will not have to take a bad grade on your midterms, Brian."

"You don't know how bad I am in these subjects," Brian replied ruefully.

"Someone once said to me, nothing beats a failure but a try," said Rit, standing his ground.

"My father has said that from time to time, so it sounds funny coming from a young man, but still true. Okay," agreed Brian, "Where are we going?"

"You pick," said Rit, tucking his skateboard under his arm.

"The quietest place I can think of, with the fewest distractions, is the library at my house."

They quickly agreed on that destination and headed for the parking lot to get Brian's car.

❊ | ❊

So intent were they on their purpose, Rit and Brian didn't notice the young woman with curly blonde hair standing near the administration building. She, however, saw them and gave a brief nod of her head—a kind of "thought so!" look. Then she spotted her sister and their new friend Greg approaching and waved.

"How was your day?" Greg asked. Bunny shrugged her shoulders and smiled blandly as if her day had been pretty much like any other, but Grace noticed a vibrancy that had been missing from her sister's personality for years. She credited their new acquaintance with drawing out the more-animated Bunny. Had Grace known about the tiny spark of interest in a certain young Asian man, she might have added that factor. As it was, Bunny kept most of her world undisclosed, even to Grace, though now a small crack was appearing in her wall of privacy.

"I was thinking—" started Greg.

Bunny opened her eyes very wide and placed her hand over her mouth as if shocked. Both Grace and Greg caught the joke, laughing.

"Very funny. Thinking is something I do on occasion," Greg retorted, grinning. "On this particular occasion, I was considering the fact that I have a car."

The girls looked at each other and then at Greg. Grace said, "Great!" and Bunny nodded enthusiastically. Over the last couple of days, this young man had started turning the fortresses that restricted their lives to dust.

Greg offered them each an arm as he had the previous evening and escorted them to his vehicle.

"Nice," remarked Grace, feeling that she should properly admire it.

Bunny nodded approvingly as Greg held the passenger door open then climbed in back before Grace settled in front.

Taking the driver's seat, Greg started the engine and then looked at Grace with his eyebrows raised as if to say, "Do you know how good that engine sounds?"

Grace didn't know anything about cars but understood his expression and met his eyes, her head sagely nodding. "We live out a ways," she warned.

"Must be a long bus ride," he rejoined. "Would you mind if I stop at my place first? It's not very far." Greg smiled. "I live within walking distance, but I love to drive my car to school in the morning."

Grace glanced at Bunny, who shrugged her unconcern. "No problem," she told Greg. Actually, she was glad he'd suggested it. She was curious about this young man—where he lived, what kind of family he had.

Greg drove a couple blocks left and then one right. A big church came into view.

"Oh, that's a beautiful church!" remarked Grace.

"You should hear its bells. You strike me as someone who would really love them," Greg said without offering any explanation of just what made him think that.

Then they pulled up in front of his house, a roomy Victorian, complete with a round, tower-like projection on the corner, on an old tree-shaded street lined with other homes of similar vintage.

"Here we are," Greg said. "Would you care to come in? I just want to drop off my books, pick up a sweater, and grab us some sodas, but why don't you come on in and meet my mom?"

Grace's first look around as she got out of the car took in the home, for *home* it was, not just a house. White and bearing graceful gingerbread ornamentation that softened its bulk and with well-tended shrubbery and flower beds along its foundation, it also had a deep porch across the front and around a corner, outfitted with comfortable-looking chairs and a glider. Noting the shade provided by a towering oak in the front yard, Grace thought, *That would be a wonderful place to sit, even on a hot summer day.* Overall, she thought this home said "Welcome" even before the door opened. It also had a look of permanence and dependability to it. And based on what she knew of him so far, Grace thought it fit him perfectly.

Grace suddenly realized Bunny hadn't even moved yet to get out of the car. She just sat there staring with a look on her face that even Grace couldn't quite read.

"Bunny, are you coming in?"

Her attention regained, Bunny nodded and stepped out of the car with an odd smile on her face, joining Grace in following Greg up the walk. Then when they got to the porch, she surprised her sister by stepping past her and Greg and ringing the doorbell.

7

Brian pulled up in the circular driveway and parked to one side. Rit ducked his head to peer out the car's front window and with an exaggerated motion moved his eyes up slowly to the roof of Brian's house.

Brian chuckled. "Come on in," he invited, getting out of the car and leading the two up the drive toward the house.

Rit, like most comedians at heart, responded to laughter with even more antics. He pretended great caution while getting out of the vehicle and placed one foot in front of the other in mock trepidation all the way up the drive until the two stopped in the porte-cochere that framed the front entrance. When Rit got to this point, he simply forgot about clowning and turned slowly to look all about him, from the tall, carved door around to the meticulously laid out garden to the ancient collection of trees in the arboretum, with his mouth slightly open in awe. Graceful statues and a small, sparkling fountain further adorned the garden, and stone benches were strategically placed along its gravel walkways so that one might sit and take in the beauty. Though most of the flowers were by now past their bloom, a blaze of artfully arranged mums brightened the autumn scene, and birds twittered around a sprinkling of feeders that hung on graceful wrought-iron poles around the garden's perimeter and under the nearest trees.

"You should see this place in the spring," Brian remarked.

"Just from what I can see now, I'd say your gardener is really an artist," Rit commented. "This is beautiful!"

"Would you like to sit out here while we study?"

"Too distracting," Rit replied. "Better go with the original plan."

When they entered the foyer, Rit noticed that Brian picked up the little card in the bouquet on the table and murmured under his breath, "She hasn't read this, so she must be delayed somewhere." With a sigh, he stuck the card back into the arrangement and led Rit into the dining room. He pointed out a tray of homemade cookies and assorted pieces of fruit sitting on the sideboard, along with a couple of insulated beverage carafes, cups and saucers, small plates, and some napkins. He offered with seamless grace, "Help yourself to refreshments. One of the carafes will have coffee in it, and the other probably has something like hot cider."

"No, thank you," Rit responded politely.

"Hey, do make yourself comfortable, okay? You don't have to be so formal. Make yourself at home, Rit. The library is through those doors and around the corner, if you'd like to explore. Please excuse me. I won't be but a couple of minutes." Then holding up one finger, he moved away toward the drawing room, where he sat down next to a small telephone table, picked up the phone, and started punching buttons, making a few notes as he listened. When he was done, he stuffed one message slip in his pocket and slipped the others into the appropriate slots in a small rack beside the phone.

Meanwhile Rit, who at sixteen didn't need too much persuasion to eat, picked out a small bunch of grapes and a couple of cookies, poured himself some cider, and settling his book bag over one shoulder, found his way to the library.

He stepped through the double doors then stopped and gazed around him at the walls of books, the big stone fireplace, and the comfortable-looking club chairs arranged beside it. Afternoon sunlight streamed through the tall windows framed in velvet drapes now pulled back, giving all a soft glow. "Wow," he murmured to himself, "a guy could get used to living like this." Then he carefully made his way across the thick oriental carpet to a seat at a heavy oak library table in the middle of the room, taking extra care not to spill anything as he walked.

When Brian returned, carrying his own cup and a couple of cookies in one hand and his briefcase in the other, he found Rit contentedly munching while he admired the oil painting over the fireplace of a Colorado mountain scene. Brian opened his briefcase and laid his books, notebook, and pens and pencils out before them.

"Ready?" he asked.

"Yep," the younger man responded, pulling a calculator and pencil out of his own book bag. "Let's take a look at the subject of your first midterm exam, okay?"

Brian was impressed with Rit's ability to get right down to business. Except for the moment it took Brian to return to the dining room, bringing the snack tray to the library and placing it within their reach, the two young men concentrated on the subjects at hand until the lights started coming on. The first one made Rit jump.

"It's on a timer and motion sensor," Brian explained to put Rit at ease.

Rit looked at his watch with surprise. "How long do you want to study?"

"As long as you do, but I think we could adjourn to the dining room for dinner," Brian responded.

"One more hour should get you a good grade in calc, Brian. I should use your phone, though, if I'm going to stay for dinner."

Brian went over to an extension beside one of the fireside chairs and, pressing the intercom button, notified the cook that there would be a guest. Then he got an outside line for Rit and held out the phone to him, stepping away so Rit could call his mother.

While Rit was on the phone, Brian went back to his studies with admirable tenacity. When Rit returned to the table, he asked Brian a couple of questions, and then, satisfied that Brian was all set on his excursion into mathematics land, he turned to his own homework. Rit had opened up a new perception of an old horizon, and he could tell Brian was enjoying it. The thought put an odd little smile on his face as his eyes moved rapidly across the pages.

A grandfather clock somewhere in the house rang six times, and Brian stretched, taking a long breath as if coming up from deep water. Rit stopped reading and looked inquiringly at Brian with raised eyebrows and a smile.

"Okay, how about a break?" Brian suggested.

Dinner was excellent, but the ambiance was strange for Rit. He joked about the two of them not having enough elbowroom at the eight-foot-long table. Brian replied that there was less than usual, cluing in Rit to the fact that most of his meals were taken alone. Making no rejoinder this time, Rit just gave him a serious, measuring look.

After they ate, they continued their studies in the library until almost at the same time, Brian arrived at a satisfactory stopping point and Rit finished all his homework.

"Thank you so much, Rit," Brian said, standing up.

"You're very welcome," Rit replied. "This is a great place to study. That was a wonderful dinner too! Thanks."

"You're also very welcome. Would you like to see the rest of the place?"

"Would I?" Rit responded enthusiastically, and off they went. He got a tour, family stories at his insistence, and some kind of frothy dessert at the end of it all.

Then the two walked out on the grounds for a while, this time around the end of the house and toward the rear of the property. There was a pond, and around its edge, ducks were sitting with their heads under their wings. Lights glowed softly here and there, lighting up bushes or picturesque groups of trees. A surrealistic, huge moon completed the scene, giving it almost more the appearance of a painting than real life.

"No more gnats at this time of year," Brian commented.

"Nope." Rit didn't try to make conversation; nor did Brian, each just relaxing and enjoying the moment and the company. Brian stood quietly and felt uplifted by their peaceful surroundings.

After a bit Rit sighed and stretched. "I guess I'd better get home," he said. As Brian reached in his pocket for his keys, Rit added, "I need to grab my backpack, though. I left it back where we were studying."

"The car's still out front, but we can cut through the house on the way," Brian replied and led Rit to a patio he hadn't noticed before, through a set of French doors, and back into the library. As they walked toward the car, Rit's steps slowed and he started walking backward to capture the majesty of the mansion in the evening light.

When Rit reached the car, Brian was sitting in the front seat with the dome light on. As Rit opened the passenger door and got in, Brian was putting something back into his pocket. He reached out his hand once Rit had buckled his seat belt and said, "Here you go. I hope this will be acceptable," and handed Rit a one hundred-dollar bill.

"Too much, man!" Rit exclaimed.

"No way," Brian disagreed.

"Yes, way," Rit insisted, and they both laughed.

Brian simply started the car and started down the long drive and then spoke softly but firmly. "I could make you listen to a long speech about how much it means to me to finally get a grasp of my most difficult subjects, but I won't do that to you if you'll accept what I consider to be just payment. Actually, some tutors get quite a bit of money."

"They're usually older, and that's all they do for a living," Rit argued.

Even in the dimness of the car, Rit could see Brian's dark eyes cast him a concerned look. It crossed Rit's mind that Brian might have picked up on his anxiety about putting a budding friendship into a more businesslike category. Brian was thoughtfully quiet as he pulled out into the street and started across town.

Rit just sat there holding the bill with only two fingers.

When Brian noticed this, he used it for an opportunity to change the mood. "Hey, I didn't dip that in anthrax. Why don't you put it in your pocket? Also, I consider you my new friend, not a hired hand or anything."

"Well…okay. Thanks, Brian." Rit finally relaxed and stuck the money into his own wallet, twisting in the seat to reach his hip pocket.

"You're worth it." There was a warm glow in Rit's heart that Brian's assessment of his awkward moment had been correct, and his respect for Brian's character grew.

Turning back to more casual conversation, Brian started talking with Rit about school, and one thing led to another. Before they got to Rit's home, Brian had learned quite a few things about Rit's grandfather, the family's life in Taiwan, their move to America, their time in Boston, and finally their move to Denver.

When they pulled up to the curb in front of Rit's house, the two thanked each other again as Brian popped the trunk so Rit could retrieve his skateboard.

⊰ 팈 | 팈 ⊱

After Brian drove away, Rit stood outside his house for a while. He felt good, really good. He was going to go inside and tell his parents about the new arrangement with Brian. Then he would give his mother the money he'd earned tonight, enjoying the look on her face.

When Rit eventually did go in, everything went exactly the way he'd imagined it would—Rit's mother beamed at him and his father nodded proudly. "What an unreal day!" he told himself as he started up the stairs to his room.

Before he got very far, the phone in the hallway rang, and he jumped back down three stairs to answer it. As it turned out, the call was for him. It was the woman from the school system who had hooked him up with the university, and she was inviting him and his family to a late fall barbeque. He asked her to wait briefly while he checked with his parents, who agreed. Rit thanked her for the invitation and accepted happily. Once he had hung up, he took an agenda book out of his backpack and carefully made an entry on the appropriate date before heading back up the stairs.

"My social life has improved two hundred percent in just twenty-four hours," was the final calculation of his most incredible day.

8

After a brief delay, the door was opened by a middle-aged woman, her neat, black slacks and soft grey blouse topped by a bright print apron. Her still-youthful face quickly broke into a surprised smile.

"Why, hello, Bunny! I didn't expect to see you now. How nice!" She reached behind her to untie the apron and pull it off as she pushed the screen door wide open. "Come on in. I was just getting something in the oven for dinner tonight." She paused to look more closely at Bunny, a slight look of concern on her face. "Is everything okay?"

Bunny nodded as she entered ahead of the others, a mischievous smile beginning to grow. Now looking a bit confused, the woman looked up at her son as he followed Bunny in, starting to ask, "Greg! What—" but her half-spoken query was met by equal confusion on Greg's face.

Grace stepped in behind Greg, her face showing her own hesitant confusion, and when Bunny took a look at her sister, her face broke into a wide grin. Turning to Greg, his mother asked, "How do you know Bunny? I didn't think you had ever met her."

"Actually, Mom, I just met these wonderful young women, and I brought them here to meet you."

"Well, Bunny and I have known each other for a long time now, but I've never met this young woman." Turning to Grace, she added, "You must be Bunny's sister, though, Grace. We've spoken on the phone before, but it's very nice to have the chance to meet you in person." Mrs. Johnson reached out to shake hands with Grace.

"Yes, ma'am, I'm Bunny's sister," Grace responded, taking her hand. "Pleased to meet you." She smiled for the first time and relaxed just a bit, but her face betrayed that she was still a little mystified.

"Well, this is a real surprise, but a nice one. Why don't you call me Violet, if you like?" Then turning to include the others, Mrs. Johnson added, "Would you like to come back to the kitchen and have a snack? We can talk and sort out just how this happened." Greg followed his mother and his new friends to the kitchen, still looking a bit bewildered. Each of them took seats at the table while Violet Johnson removed the thick glass cover from the cake stand on the counter, revealing a delicious-looking coffeecake.

"Another?" Violet softly inquired of Bunny. Bunny gave a little nod.

Another? Thought Greg, *Meaning she must have had a first. Meaning she must have been here earlier. Meaning she must be the girl that Mom works with.* He glanced up to look directly into his mother's amused eyes. She had thrown him the clue on purpose. He smiled gratefully. He didn't like being the only person out of the loop. *And here is a chance to impress Grace with my great mind,* he joked to himself and said aloud, "So you are Mom's mystery student."

Bunny nodded as she accepted a slice of cake and set the dish down in front of her.

Grace started to make a comment but was interrupted by the telephone ringing. Violet got up to answer it, gently holding up her hand as a non-verbal request for a pause. After only a brief exchange with the caller, her pleasant tone changed abruptly, as did the expression on her face, and she hung up, stepping quickly over to the radio.

Our little radio is getting quite a bit more use lately, Greg observed silently as his mother turned up the volume so all could hear.

"…video passed on today to the U.S. ambassador in Baghdad. The White House says it shows the last words of Steven Hadley, the kidnapped CNN reporter. The video also contained graphic scenes showing the torture, abuse, and execution-style shooting of Hadley. At the end of the tape, in addition to repeating earlier demands, there was a threatening message directed at the president of the United States."

Violet turned off the radio with a click. There was not a single sound in the kitchen.

"I think we should pray," said Greg, breaking the silence with the ultimate suggestion.

"Good idea," his mother responded quickly.

The girls looked at each other. But each then just diffidently bowed her head and closed her eyes, politely following the lead of their host and hostess. Their manner told Violet and Greg that perhaps the girls had little if any religious instruction, particularly in a prayerful response to traumatic situations.

Greg jumped right in though. "Thank you, God, for always hearing us when we pray. You have a plan for the nations. You have a plan to save all the people of the world through your Son, Jesus, and his atoning sacrifice. We will trust you now, even though the world situation looks like it is spinning out of control. We will call You our strong rock, and we believe in times of trouble You will deliver us. Bless the family of that reporter who was a martyr for our nation. Comfort them in their loss, and provide for the family like the father they lost. Thank you for being our Father, loving and good. Amen."

"Amen," said Violet. Then, having caught the girls' initial hesitation, she continued, "Would anyone like something to drink with the rest of your cake? Milk? Tea?"

"I think Bunny would like a glass of milk, and I would love a cup of tea," Grace replied eagerly, obviously glad for the quick diversion.

Grace had spoken for Bunny concerning beverages, but something happened just then that no one was expecting. Bunny was in the same bowed position, but her eyes were open as if looking at the table in front of her. They were not focused on the table, however, and her mouth was slightly ajar, as if she were astounded. Grace leaned over, her hand outstretched to lightly shake Bunny's shoulder, but Violet held up that instructive hand again, silently causing Grace to pause.

"I think God may be showing her something special," Violet said softly. "Why don't we let Him finish?"

Grace dropped her hand but then froze, looking at Violet as if she couldn't quite take in what was being said.

Catching her confusion, Greg decided to intervene. "Grace?" He also spoke quietly. "Could I speak with you privately?"

She looked as though she didn't want to leave her sister alone in the kitchen, but after a moment's hesitation, nodded assent and rose to follow Greg out of the room.

He led her through the dining room to a bright sunroom. Decorated just right to make people feel comfortable, it was filled with pastel colors and lots of big pillows placed on the furniture.

"Come on, sit down," Greg said, gesturing to an overstuffed chair. When Grace snuggled into the big chair, he asked, "Just how freaked out are you at this point?"

She responded with a short, breathy laugh, and then her features fell back into a puzzled look.

"Could I ask you what religious background you have? It would help me know how to explain," Greg plunged on.

"Actually, none," Grace replied. "Church wasn't ever part of our life, and I don't remember either my mother or my aunt ever talking about God or praying or anything like that."

"Okay." Greg took a breath and started in. "It talks in the Bible, in the old Jewish scriptures—the Old Testament—especially, about people having dreams and visions from God. In short, that is probably what your sister is experiencing right now. In this house we believe in God and have asked the Spirit of God to live with us." Seeing Grace's brow furrow a bit, Greg hastened to add, "We aren't involved with a cult or anything way out there. Don't worry about that." Greg grinned. "When you come right down to it, my family is fairly normal. We have ups and downs like most other people. We are certainly not very extreme in any way." Greg continued gently. "The only extraordinary thing about us, in fact, is God working in our lives, which continuously astounds even us."

Grace responded as though she could tell how much he wanted her to accept his family and their ways. "It's all right, Greg, I get it. You don't seem weird to me, just funny and nice."

Nice? Wonderful. Now I seem "nice." Warning, warning! Ship going down, Greg thought, but aloud he said calmly, "Would you like that tea now, Grace? I could bring it to you here or we could return to the kitchen. Whatever you want."

Grace nodded and attempted to get out of the chair, but she'd sunk so deeply into it that she fell backward again. She and Greg laughed together. Dropping his voice into a spooky bass, he intoned, "A chair designed to keep you here…forever." Then he laughed again and extended his hand to help her up.

Grace accepted the assist and responded, "Well, you're too much of a nut to be some kind of dark religious extremist!"

The atmosphere lightened, and the two returned to the kitchen. They found Bunny drawing on a piece of paper, her untouched cake pushed aside. Other sketches lay on the table. Bunny was concentrating so completely on her sketching that she didn't even look up as they entered the room, or even as they took their seats. She seemed in a hurry, as if she would forget something important if she didn't draw it quickly. Yet she didn't seem ruffled, only determined.

Violet, who had been sitting back quietly, just watching, picked up one of the drawings and handed it to Grace and Greg. Though they might only have been curious at first, the two quickly leaned in to look more closely. Grace's mouth involuntarily dropped open, and she reached for another of the growing pile of sketches.

9

The first picture was a very clear drawing of some young men shooting at a pedestrian from their car. The bullets were depicted as actually entering a house behind the person on foot. The picture also showed an overturned bed and people crowded into a corner behind a large dresser inside the house. The boy in the picture, who was shielding the others, had clear and well-defined Asian features.

Grace had always known that Bunny had artistic talent, but now her work seemed especially adept as it worked with this newly discovered gift. Grace reached for another sketch. Glancing at Greg as she did so, she saw that he was still studying the first picture. *He probably never thought the afternoon would go like this!* she thought, though she noted that this family seemed quite open to surprises from God.

Looking down at the new drawing she had picked up, Grace froze. It was an unmistakable portrait of the nation's president, who was being threatened and harassed, not by people, but by ugly creatures flying in the air all around him. One being had a glass vial in its hand, and on the vial was the tiny figure of a human covered with small spots. Another creature had a bowl heaped up with dust, and on the bowl was a minute illustration of a person apparently choking or struggling to breathe. A third demon—for that's what these clearly were—was holding a bomb-like device, and a fourth held several human puppets on strings whose poses indicated suicidal intentions. There was another terrible-looking creature that didn't have anything in its hands but was pointing with one finger at the president and seemed to be urging the others on with the other hand. Grace laid this drawing in front of Greg and reached for another.

This one had two parts, two rooms divided by a thin wall. In the first room was the president, now seated at his desk with his hand on his forehead as if it hurt. The second room contained a lot of people. At first glance, the scene looked like a joyous party, but when Grace looked more carefully, she could see that the people's faces didn't look very happy, and they were all doing mean or self-indulgent things. The woman by the punch bowl was holding her glass and smiling, but she was also standing on the foot of the man who was talking to her. There was a lovely couple with their arms around each other's waists, but then Grace saw that the man was exchanging a promising look with another woman over his wife's head, and she was giving another man across the room a sexy smile. Off to one side someone was piling high all the party food they could possibly get onto one plate, and elsewhere a man was putting a statue from a table under his coat. There were also people ignoring all the others, watching television in the corner. And no one in the whole room seemed to notice or care what might be going on with their president right in the next room.

The next sketch showed a woman tied up in a corner. There were several others similarly bound, but they had been turned so they faced the wall. Only her face could be seen, and every detail of it showed shock and fear. Sitting at a distance from the captives, faces averted, were two unbound men wearing Middle Eastern dress. There was a fire in the middle of the picture, with two partially burned books on its perimeter. In very small letters, one was labeled *Koran* and the other said *Bible*. In the upper portion of the drawing, Bunny had put angels with their hands stretched toward the little group on the floor and wings spread like a feathery covering over them.

When Bunny finished her last sketch, she laid down her pencil and reached out her hand for the others and began to arrange all in some private order. Greg dug around in his book bag for an empty folder. Not finding one, he emptied a folder he was using for one of his courses and handed it to Bunny. She smiled her thanks and carefully placed all the sketches inside. Grace noticed that her sister had very definitely not shown the last sketch to anyone, but though she was very curious, she said nothing.

Violet was the first to speak. "What an afternoon this turned out to be!"

Greg and Grace agreed solemnly and Bunny nodded her head. No one seemed to want to make a further contribution.

Then Violet changed the subject. "I'm trying to put together a barbeque for next Saturday. Do you girls think you can make it? Greg, what does your calendar look like?"

She continued describing the menu and expressing hope for good weather while Greg again dug through his bag, this time for his planner. His mother had finished her part of the conversation and the girls had responded affirmatively by the time Greg finally found what he'd been searching for. He triumphantly held up the little book while Grace smiled and his mother ruefully shook her head.

"Looks good, Mom," he announced after leafing through the pages. Then he turned to Grace and Bunny and said, "If you girls need to get home, I'll take you now. Or do you need to use the phone?" His voice faltered slightly as he continued, "Please stay as long as you like, but I'm feeling a little awkward because I initially told you I only wanted to grab some sodas and drop off my books."

"I don't think you planned all of this to keep us here this afternoon, Greg," returned Grace in good humor. "It's up to Bunny." Turning to her sister, she asked, "Do you want to stay?"

Hesitating, Bunny looked at Violet, who suggested, "Maybe you could help me with the rest of my plans for the party. Would you like to do that?" Bunny smiled and nodded. "Could you two stay for supper?" Violet asked.

Grace jested, "If Greg won't start to think it's his new job to feed us." Greg waved the quip off while his mother gave him a quizzical look, though without comment.

"Come on, comedienne, I'll show you the rest of the house," he invited, and Grace rose and disappeared with him for the next hour.

Violet first made a call to her husband, letting him know they had two guests. After talking with him for just a few minutes, she hung up and turned to Bunny. "The main part of dinner is already in the oven, and Carl said he'd stop on the way home and get something to go with it, so all we need to do now is think about that barbeque. Let's go to the study where all my files are."

In the familiar room where the two spent so many afternoons, Violet pulled a folder labeled *Fall Party* from her file cabinet and selected a pen from the container on her desk before taking a seat in the easy chair next to Bunny's. Bunny looked at her with eyebrows raised high and a little smile. "Well if I didn't organize absolutely everything, I would forget important details." Bunny made a funny little face in response, and then together they got to work on their planning.

⚜|⚜

All in all, the girls had a wonderful evening with Greg and his parents. Carl Johnson was a tall, outgoing man with a great sense of humor. He was built like a linebacker and could no doubt look fearsome when getting serious about business, but privately he proved to be thoughtful and caring. Now fifty-two, he had just recently retired after thirty years on the Denver police force.

The numerous pictures and award plaques displayed prominently on the walls of the Johnson home hinted at how important to the whole family his career had been. In fact, Greg's sister, who was several years older than Greg, had followed in her father's footsteps and was now on a specialized service team of the NYPD. In fact, the family suffered a particular scare on 9/11, fearing that she might have been killed when the planes flown by suicidal fanatics had demolished the World Trade Center, killing people from around the world that were doing business on that day. It was two days before the Johnsons finally learned that she had been injured in the disaster but was alive, undergoing treatment at a New York City hospital. She received honors for her service on that terrible day, and after several months' leave for recovery, she had been able to return to work.

As she sat curled up by the fireplace after dinner, Grace felt all warm and cheery inside and out. Looking around her, she thought about the evening. *It's hard to believe any family can be like this—so caring about each other, so nice to us, so much fun. And it's peaceful in this house, even with five people around.*

⇥|⇤

Grace was surprised when Greg pulled up in front of their house; the ride had gone so quickly as they talked about this and that.

When Greg helped them out of the car and began walking them to the front door, Grace wasn't really paying attention, still enthralled by the spectacular day. Then Bunny started pulling at her sleeve. When Grace turned to see what she wanted, Bunny vehemently shook her head no.

"What?" Grace asked.

Bunny gestured toward the back of the house.

"Do you know how silly that would look to him?" Grace replied in a hushed voice.

"How silly?" Greg too had stopped to see what was going on and was now right at Grace's side.

Bunny folded her arms, looking immovable.

Grace looked from her to Greg and moaned in exasperation, "Oh, okay. Come this way, Greg." After leading the others around to the back of the house, she dug around in her backpack until she found her keys. Unlocking the French doors and reaching inside to flip on a light, then stepping aside to let Bunny in, she turned to face Greg, feeling sheepish.

"I'm not even going to ask," was his jocular comment.

Grace was beginning to appreciate this young man more every moment. The admiration on her face suddenly made her so endearing that Greg drew her into a spontaneous embrace. She let him hold her close for a long moment and then she stepped back. Stooping down to pick up her backpack, she thanked him for "just everything."

As she stepped through the French doors into their bedroom, he asked, "One question. You *do* actually live here, right?"

Grace laughed, missing her step and almost falling back out the door. Greg took her hand to steady her. "We live here," she answered as he reluctantly let go. "Good night, Greg."

"Good night. See you tomorrow," he said and was gone into the night shadows.

After a bit, as the girls lay in their beds in the darkened room, Grace's voice floated out. "Yes, I like him."

10

R it felt like he had just gotten to sleep when a horrible dream woke him up. The house looked just the same as usual, but there was a strange atmosphere, a kind of tension in the air. Rit sat up in bed, threw back the covers, and swung his feet to the floor. But instead of standing immediately, he just sat on the edge of the bed, listening in the dark. He felt an urgent need to run down the stairs to his parents' bedroom but resisted it. He heard the sound of a car with a bad muffler coming down the street toward their house and again stopped himself from running downstairs. The feeling was so strong that he grabbed the bedding to hold himself in place. Then he heard rapid gunfire, and there was the sound of someone running on the pavement outside, yelling, and finally the loud muffler faded into the night. Rit instantly felt as if he were unlocked, now able to move. He hurried out of his room, down the stairs, and then through the house to his parents' room, and against his earlier reservations, he opened their door without knocking. A horrible sight met his eyes. He squeezed them tightly shut so that he could no longer see it. *It's my fault, but I couldn't let myself go down the stairs. Why did I stop the impulse to run to them? If I hadn't, they would be alive now! It's my fault…* Rit's thoughts began to repeat in an odd way, and the feelings of horror and calamity swirled around him. He felt they would swallow him, and he gasped for air, fighting the feeling of being unable to breathe.

Then he woke up.

Rit sat up in bed, placing his feet on the floor but then sitting on the edge of the bed and just listening in the dark. He felt an urgent need to run down the stairs to his parents' bedroom and instantly bolted out of his room, down the stairs, and through the house to their room. He threw open the door without knocking and loudly and insistently demanded that they get out of their beds onto the floor. As he spoke, Rit heard a car with a loud muffler approaching. His startled parents rolled out of bed onto the floor. Their bed sat right under a window facing the street, and Rit hastily lifted the mattress and shoved it up to cover the window, all the while urgently telling his parents to get behind the big bureau in the corner. Still completely stunned, they complied without questions, and Rit piled into the corner with them just as shots from an automatic weapon came through the window. Running feet. Yelling. He could hear all the noises from his dream like background effects from some action movie.

When the usual relative quiet resumed, Rit unfolded himself from around his parents and went into the family room, dropping into the first available chair. His knees were shaking uncontrollably.

A short time later, he felt rather than saw or heard his father come into the room, still so enveloped in the trauma was he. Mr. Han turned on a light and sat down in a chair across from his son, adjusting his navy blue bathrobe around him. When Rit looked up, he saw something he'd never ever seen before, tears glistening in his father's eyes. They didn't actually roll down his cheeks, but they were quite discernibly there before he blinked a few times, and then they were gone.

Mr. Han cleared his throat as if to speak just as Rit's mother, also in bathrobe and slippers, came in with a tray holding cups and saucers and a steaming pot of tea. As she quietly went about pouring a cup for each of them, Mr. Han made another attempt to speak. "How did you know to do that, son?"

"I had a dream, Father," Rit replied, hesitating, wondering how much to say.

The parents exchanged a look as Mrs. Han brought a cup of tea to each of them. The scent of jasmine calmed Rit as his mother had hoped it would, and she nodded at her husband, indicating her approval of the unspoken thing that had passed between them.

"When did you start having such vivid dreams?" Rit's father inquired in Chinese.

Also reverting to their mother tongue in this shaken moment, Rit replied, "I have had dreams as long as I can remember, Father." He thought it was also unusual that his dad got right to the point and attributed this to either the late hour or the possible import of the conversation. He decided to ask, "Is this significant?"

Rit's mother placed her hand on his cheek and looked meaningfully at her husband then picked up her own cup and retired.

Still in Mandarin, Rit's dad informed him that important dreams were given to all the men in his line. Every generation had a Han man who had dreams that warned them of upcoming events. With this gift came a responsibility, the challenge to develop and use the gift for the benefit of others. "As you have done, son," Rit's father stated. "You may even have sensed in one of your dreams what could happen if you do not choose active involvement."

Rit felt overwhelmed, similar to the dreadfulness of his dream, but without the violence and self-recrimination. He wanted to tell his father how exactly right he was, especially regarding that last statement, but the thought of having to relive even part of that horrible dream, even through the telling of it, was beyond his capability just then. He passed his hand over his face in a disconcerted fashion, and his father immediately stood up.

"Good night, son. You have saved our life tonight, you and the giver of this gift you have."

Rit stood up. After looking into his son's eyes for a long moment, Mr. Han left to join his wife in the guest room he knew she'd made up for them. Rit sat back down momentarily. Then feeling very alone and still overwhelmed by all that had occurred, he went back upstairs to work on his computer.

Sitting down at his desk and booting up the computer, he pulled up a program that had a particularly good mind teaser, hoping to be able to focus and then become immersed in his schoolwork, but he found it hard to concentrate. The evening's events replayed in his mind until he finally just shut down the computer and went back down the stairs to his parents' bedroom.

Hoping to find some closure to the episode, he quietly lowered the mattress back onto the bed. When he did so, he saw the holes, maybe a dozen or more, and the harsh awareness of his parents' narrow escape from death increased. Even living on the cusp between a rather bad part of town and a respectable neighborhood where gun shots were heard from time to time didn't diminish the shock of a random act of violence happening to one's own family. He knew there wouldn't be further activity around the house now though, as his parents had chosen not to draw more attention to their home at this juncture by calling the police, but probably would report the incident quietly later on that day. Rit pulled the ruined bottom sheet off the mattress and then gathered the rest of the bedding, now tangled at the foot of the bed. Getting clean sheets from the closet, Rit carefully remade the bed and then fell to his knees beside it, not knowing what to do or think or feel. He had never experienced such empty confusion. He laid his head on the bed.

Sometime during the night he crawled up into the bed, pulling a blanket partially over him and slept without further dreams.

11

Morning brought sunbeams of happiness, or such was Grace's impression as she got ready for her morning classes. Bunny too seemed content; gone was the blank apathy that had been overcoming her personality. The girls even went through the house, waving cheerful good-byes to everyone, and used the front door to leave. They parted ways at the corner. Grace's step was so light she was all but skipping as she headed for the bus stop and her day on campus. She waved at Bunny, who was cheerfully trotting toward her own school.

⊰|⊱

Rit was awakened by a tickling sensation on his face and became aware that he was cold. Opening his eyes, he saw that the window curtains were lifting out over the bed away from a window that was now mostly a gaping hole, jagged shards clinging to the battered sash around the emptiness through which the nippy, October morning breeze was blowing. It was a corner of a waving curtain that had brushed over his face.

"This is not a good way to start the day," Rit commented to himself, but once he was on his feet, he had to admit that he felt better after getting some sleep. Yet he was *cold*, and he hurried out of the room, quickly closing the door, and dashed back upstairs to his own room.

When he'd taken a hot shower, dressed, and gathered up his books, he headed back downstairs. He'd have to hurry this morning. He was running late now, but he stopped in the kitchen before heading out the door. What relief he felt just seeing his mom busily working there, just as on any other day! He startled her slightly by giving her a big, spontaneous hug. Then he looked past her to see what she was busy making and saw the growing array of spring rolls on the counter. "Those look wonderful, Mother."

"I thought this would be a good day to make something special for you and your father." She smiled gently at him then, her eyes showing that she was remembering what a unique night it had been for them all.

"I'm sorry I can't sit down for breakfast today. I've got to hurry so I won't be late for school."

"You must have something to eat, Rit. At least take two with you," she said, retrieving two rolls from beside the stove and wrapping them in a napkin handed them to him.

"Thank you, Mother," He said, accepting the food and heading toward the door. "I'll see you this afternoon. Bye." Rit dashed out of the house, grabbed Ruby from the porch, and then rolled down the driveway and out into the street gingerly nibbling on a steaming spring roll as he went.

⊰ | ⊱

After attending his scheduled classes at the high school, Rit took a slower route than usual to the university to meet Brian. When he spotted a towering steeple nearby, he detoured slightly to approach it. He had noticed it many times before, but today he felt strangely drawn to investigate. When he actually got to the church—a lovely, stone, English, gothic edifice—he discovered that it was much larger than it looked from a distance. He rolled up its front drive toward the entry before stopping Ruby and stepping off to pause and look up. As Rit gazed all the way up to the top of the cross on the steeple, he felt small, very small, and something else that was not at all unpleasant.

Carefully parking Ruby under a nearby shrub, Rit pushed open one of the heavy, polished doors and peered inside. The bright sun outside made it hard for his eyes to adjust to the comparative darkness inside, but as he looked across the narthex and into the long nave, he marveled at the myriad colors from all the stained glass windows—how they all collided and mingled on the walls and carpeting.

As he entered and quietly crossed the narthex, he was struck by the hushed peacefulness in this place. Then after a brief hesitation, he stepped through the archway into the rear of the nave. As his eyes traveled slowly down the long row of pews, their finish softly reflecting the colors falling from the side windows, and onto the chancel and the glorious rose window high in its outer wall, a feeling of welcome pervaded his soul. Rit continued slowly toward the front, where a single candle burned on the altar, a tall cross rising above it. He stood near the communion rail, allowing his soul the refreshment he found in the tranquil surroundings.

〜❖|❖〜

Following her afternoon with Mrs. Johnson—Violet—
Bunny walked toward the university campus as usual
to meet up with Grace, holding her folder close to her.
She hadn't opened it since she'd placed all the drawings
inside the evening before, though she'd slept with it
under her pillow and kept it right beside her all day as
she did her schoolwork.

Violet had given Bunny a hug before she left the
house. "You are making such progress, dear girl. You
could even graduate early, if you keep up the pace."

Bunny laid her head briefly on Violet's shoulder,
something she rarely did with anyone, and then walked
down the cement walk with even more spring in her step.

Now, further down the street, she looked at her
watch, and seeing that she was a little earlier than usual,
she impulsively decided to explore the big church she'd
been noticing as she walked between the Johnson home
and the campus. Turning up the sweeping drive toward
the entry, she took in the massive stone walls and the
towering steeple as she approached. Then she pushed
open a front door and went inside.

The church felt strong to Bunny, strong and good.
Despite the way things had been improving lately, she
yearned for love and protection in her life. Her sister
had been the sole fountain of strength for Bunny, and
sometimes even Grace seemed fragile and kind of lost.
As she passed through the narthex and stepped into the
long nave of the church, Bunny immediately saw that
someone else had gotten there first.

When he turned around, she found that he mirrored the surprise she felt recognizing him. He only spoke one word, "You!" and pointed at her. Bunny pointed back at him. The two of them might have looked a little comical to an observer, both just standing there, pointing at each other in surprise.

Bunny let him approach within a few feet and then held up her hand like a police officer stopping traffic. Rit seemed to understand. Pausing, he greeted her, gave his name, and waited for her response. Bunny just stood, quietly studying his face.

"I feel like I know you," Rit tried as an opener. "That might sound like a line, but honestly, I think I had a dream about you."

If it was a line, it was the bravest one Bunny had ever heard, and considering what had happened to her just the previous afternoon, she was more inclined to believe him than she might have been before.

"Could you tell me your name?"

Bunny shook her head.

The young man's face immediately fell into one of the most dejected looks she'd ever seen. Normally such a look had no influence on Bunny, and usually Rit didn't take this type of thing to heart either, but somehow this was different to each of them.

Quite suddenly the crust around Bunny's soul gave way. She truly wanted this boy to understand, and she reached out so hesitantly that by the time her fingertips touched his sleeve, he was staring at her in a very puzzled way.

When Bunny gestured to make him understand her silence, sudden comprehension dawned on Rit's face. Always one to find a solution to any problem, he took off his backpack and got out a notepad and pen. Handing them to her, he started over. "I'm Rit, and you are?"

Bunny, she quickly wrote on the paper.

"No way," he replied.

Yes way, she wrote back.

He laughed. "I guess you do kind of look like a Bunny—no offense."

She took longer writing back. *None taken, but I don't know what you mean.*

Rit smiled approvingly with a slight lift of his eyebrows. Aloud, he rambled on, "I mean you have a fluffy look, with your curly hair and all. Oh, I don't know what I mean; I'm just trying to start a conversation," he finally admitted with a lopsided grin.

Bunny smiled back and then wrote a question. "What about that dream?"

"Would you like to sit down? I'll tell you about it, Bunny." Rit slid into one of the pews, making room for her to sit beside him. Then in the soft, colorful light, he recaptured the ethereal feeling of the dream for her even as he accurately related every detail.

When he stopped talking, there could have been an awkward silence, but Bunny's face communicated so many mixed emotions that looking at her was like watching a slide show of Bunny portraits. She was struggling with finding a way out of her self-enforced solitude, and she appreciated the obvious effort Rit was making to bridge their communication barrier. It struck her that she might not be able to talk with her voice, but she did have a response to his dream. She had something to share with him as well. Her fingers clutched the folder tighter as she stared at him intently.

When Rit glanced at his watch, Bunny was reminded that she needed to meet Grace, and she got to her feet.

"I wish I knew what you were thinking," Rit said a little sadly.

His honesty touched her deeply, but she only gave him that intense look. She didn't know it, but it was the exact expression that the dream girl had worn as she wandered elusively through his sleep.

With a slight look of renewed surprise, Rit persisted. "Could I walk with you? Where are you going? Do you live around here?"

His renewed determination made Bunny smile, and she gestured for him to join her.

⊰|⊱

When Grace and Greg came around the corner of the Administration Building, a look of amazement came to both their faces.

Grace breathed, "*This* is a first!" There was Bunny, walking toward them with a teenage boy at her side. She held her folder, and he was carrying a bright red skateboard under his arm.

Just as they reached each other but before anyone had a chance to say anything, a shout made everyone turn their heads. "Hey, Rit ! So *that's* what was taking so long!" A tall, handsome young man was jogging across the street toward them. With a deep chuckle, he approached Rit. Then glancing around at the others, he raised his eyebrows in a perplexed way. "Wait a minute. Haven't I seen all three of you somewhere just recently?"

Brian, Greg, Grace, and Bunny put the puzzle together at about the same time. Then all turned to look at Rit as Greg said, "And *that* must be the skateboard!"

Rit had no idea how the others had met but was not one to be left out of anything for too long. He stepped up, holding his skateboard out toward them in both hands, saying, "Yes, this is Ruby the Skateboard." Then he bent lower over the board and said in a higher voice, "Pleased to meet all of you, I'm sure."

Everyone laughed, and Brian said, "Sorry, Rit, I guess intros are up to me. Let's see, where do I start? Rit, this is Grace, Bunny, and…Greg, right?"

"Impressive," Greg interjected.

"I had the good fortune to meet them the other night while I was shopping. Thanks again for the tip, Greg. As you can see, it paid off. This is the friend I didn't run over with my car, Rit, one of the smartest guys I've ever met." Brian kept it short but couldn't resist teasing him a little about Bunny. "He may be even smarter than I thought to come walking up with someone as pretty as this." Brian complimented Bunny with a smile and gave Rit a roguish wink.

Usually Grace would jump in with a comment to save Bunny from the necessity of a reply, but Rit beat her to it. "She *is* pretty, Brian. I feel very lucky to meet her." Then he turned to the others. "Are you Bunny's friends, or…?"

Grace was glad Rit had used Brian's name in a sentence because she had forgotten it, and she appreciated that Rit had chosen discretion regarding Bunny's disability which she was sure he had picked up on. "I'm her sister, and Greg is a friend of the family." She had never used the phrase "friend of the family" before. It felt nice rolling off her tongue, and she looked off into the distance, savoring the moment.

It became an even nicer moment when Greg put his arm around her shoulders, giving her a side hug, and said, "Great to meet you, Rit, and to see you again, Brian. What's everybody going to do?" Greg paused and looked at Grace for a clue about how to proceed.

Grace, so unused to such closeness but finding this new situation delightful, was still basking in the warmth of Greg's embrace and felt like she could handle anything. "Why don't we all get some ice cream or something?"

Bunny and Greg looked at her in surprise, while Rit and Brian exchanged a look, sizing the situation up.

Brian took charge. "Rit and I have some things to do, but I'm in favor of taking a bit of a break after studying most of the day. How about you, Rit ?"

"Fine with me. I like ice cream." He looked at Bunny with a twinkle in his eye. "Do you like ice cream?" He knew it would be easier for her to nod yes than to try to refuse nonverbally, which could require an explanation of some sort.

As Rit expected, Bunny nodded an affirmative, and the group started walking in the general direction of the ice cream parlour, chatting and kicking fallen leaves.

Midway there, Rit slowed down the pace for Bunny and himself, carefully dropping out of earshot. "Do you mind if my friend knows that you don't speak?" he asked directly. "If you do, we could sit at a table for two."

His polite consideration was almost overwhelming after being shut in her own lonely world for so long. Bunny stopped, and the gentle sunshine of her smile at him showed how much she appreciated his concern. Rit looked a little startled but also stood taller and drew closer to her, as though to be her protective knight as they ventured forth.

Still smiling, Bunny answered by drawing a circle in the air as if it surrounded the group.

"Okay," Rit said, nodding, and he picked up the pace so they caught up with the others.

Sitting around the little Formica table and enjoying the company of this new band of comrades, Grace thought about all that she and Bunny had been missing and the unique camaraderie that had so quickly sprung up in this group. *It takes a really special collection of people to hit it off this way,* she thought.

The small talk continued with some of the usual questions about birthplaces, college majors, and goals. Politics seemed to be common ground for Greg and Brian, which gave Grace a chance to observe the communications between Bunny and her very first young man friend. This development had a flavor like sweet, tart candy for Grace, the tart portion being the sad life her sister had led until now, with absolutely no close friends, and the sweet part being able to witness her finally making a connection. *Rit seems extremely intelligent and considerate,* she thought.

Grace's rumination was interrupted by a nudge from Greg. "Beautiful dreamer, what kind of ice cream doth the fair lady favor?" Greg directed her gaze to the waitress, who stood with a pencil ready. Then, embarrassed by his little public display of silliness, he held his menu a bit higher in front of his face, but Grace ordered without missing a beat, stating that she would "liketh" a "banana spliteth," getting a laugh from the others and saving his ego.

⊰ | ⊱

In one of those unnoticed transitions that happen in conversation, the political discussion around the table merged with the events of the preceding day, and the group began to discuss visions predicting world events.

Then at one point, Bunny glanced up from her dish and she saw that everyone was looking at her. She quickly thought back on the discussion, piecing it together. *Let's see. They were talking about terrorism, weapons we have against it, how a better spy network would benefit the president, and whether psychics would help if they were dependable. The last comment was...about God.... Oh! How God gave his prophets totally dependable visions of upcoming events to help the kings win their battles.* Bunny felt relieved that she had gotten herself up to speed, but the relief slowly changed to anxiety and then became something close to panic. Greg and Grace hadn't directly mentioned the incident with her vision, but she now realized that she was being called upon to make a contribution. *I'm not God's prophet,* she protested to herself. *It isn't like the fate of the world depends on me!* Her fingers tightened on the folder in her lap.

12

The tall, well-dressed woman pulled the card out from among the flowers. "That boy," she murmured, "he's a thoughtful one." She laid the card on the table and walked to the dining room while getting out her cell phone. Delicately picking up a few grapes from the tray on the sideboard and pouring a cup of coffee, she carried her refreshments into the drawing room, where she chose a small sofa by the window. Slipping off her high heels, she pulled a small, embroidered footstool over to her place and got comfortable, nibbling while she dialed.

"Hello?"

"Hello."

"Katherine, please, help me!"

"Meg? Is that you? You don't sound quite, yourself."

"Yes, I've been trying to phone you. Don't you forward your calls to your personal phone anymore?"

"No, I don't route my calls overseas. Brian is still here at home, but I'm home now. How are things there? I thought you were supposed to be back last week."

"That's the problem! I can't get out!"

"You can't get out? How can they keep you there? Did you go to the embassy?"

"The embassy was bombed. Someone has stolen my identification…"

"Did you try Great Britain?"

"Same thing," Meg choked out as she broke down in tears.

Mrs. Sommers fell silent then said, "Now don't cry, Meggie. We'll get you out of there. I'll make some other calls right now. Right now, okay? Okay. Got to go. Don't worry! Bye."

Her fingers trembled slightly as she took a few more grapes. She ate them distractedly and then punched some more numbers into her phone.

"Dick? We need to get someone out of the Middle East."

"Who?"

"Meg, that's who!"

Dick snorted derisively. "*That* do-gooder."

"I don't care what your opinion of her is! The world *needs* do-gooders. Is that what you call me too?"

"Certainly never, my dear Katherine."

"Oh, of course not." She indulged in a little sarcasm before taking up her friend's cause again, emphasizing every word. "Look, she's stuck there. They've taken her passport…"

"Who has taken her passport?"

"I don't know precisely who. Or even if she said who."

"Kay, it's important to know who is doing this. We really can't do anything until we know who is behind it all."

"I'm getting a bit frustrated, now. I'll call you back later, maybe. Thanks, Dick."

"What are you thanking me for?"

"Oh, I don't know…for the enlightenment? Have a good evening."

"Katherine, I wish I could have done more."

"Yes, thank you. Good-bye." Mrs. Sommers clicked off and immediately entered another number, had another dead-end conversation, and another, and one more, until she finally laid the phone on the cushion next to her, set the plate on the coffee table, and leaned back with her eyes closed.

She stayed in this position until darkness fell all around her. She was so still the room's motion detectors didn't even turn on the lights. Then finally sitting up and causing the light to spill around her, she dialed once again. "I'd like to book a flight to Riyadh, please… Yes, Saudi Arabia."

At the same time, her call waiting was beeping because Brian was desperately trying to contact his mother.

⇥|⇤

While he was together with his new friends at the ice cream parlour, Brian had seen something that changed his world. The group had paused in an odd way to look at the youngest one there, Rit's cute blonde friend, the one who hadn't said a single word the whole time they'd been at the shop. She had responded to that expectant moment only by slowly laying on the table a folder that had been in her lap. Opening it half way, she had bitten her lip for another dramatic instant before pulling out a penciled drawing and handing it to Rit. The intensity of what happened next was unforgettable for each member of the little group.

First Rit's eyes and mouth opened wide in shock as he tried and then tried again to say something.

When Rit remained silent, Grace spoke up with a question. "That's you, isn't it?"

Rit nodded and then swallowed some water from the glass in front of him before getting out, "Yes, that is my family, and that is what happened to us last night." His emotions were difficult for even him to sort out, but the group could tell that he was struggling.

Brian spoke. "We were at my place just yesterday evening!" He felt as if he had just entered the twilight zone.

"I know. I haven't had a chance to tell you about this. It happened a little after midnight."

Brian turned to Bunny. "Exactly when did you draw this picture?"

She stared at him expressively and then by habit looked at her sister for help.

Grace, caught unawares, stammered slightly. "Yesterday afternoon at Greg's house." She didn't feel it was necessary to mention the visions just yet.

"Yesterday afternoon," Brian repeated thoughtfully.

This exchange had given Rit some time to pull himself together. "So you had, what? A dream during a nap…or you just picked up a pencil and started drawing my family…" Rit let the question trail off.

"It was a vision," Greg said, jumping into the conversation. "She had a vision about many things. I guess the veracity of this vision has been proven here and now. I'm stunned myself, completely stunned."

Brian was mystified. At the same time he felt challenged to discover the deeper meaning of this "coincidental" meeting of people who were disclosing fantastic pieces of information that fit together like a mosaic. He turned back to Bunny, although he was guessing there was a reason he hadn't heard her verbalize anything yet. "You had a vision and made sketches of what you saw. And you drew something before it actually happened. Do you have more that you would let us see?"

Bunny nodded and handed all but one sketch to Brian.

After glancing at the stack of paper in his hand, he gave Bunny a friendly but questioning look as he held up the pictures. "Is there something else going on here?"

She nodded, and Rit explained, "She doesn't speak, Brian."

"Well, she certainly can draw," he said without hesitation, turning his attention back to the sketches, starting through them and looking at each one carefully. "Bunny, you are a lady with many gifts. Have you always had these visions?" He glanced at Bunny, who shook her head. "First one?" Bunny nodded. "What was it that—" His voice stopped. He was staring at the last picture Bunny had given him as if it were a poisonous insect that had just landed on the table in front of him. The others noticed and exchanged wondering looks with each other. "Please excuse me. You must excuse me. I'll be right back." Springing up from the table, Brian got out his cell phone and left the restaurant. "What now?" Greg asked with a befuddled shake of his head.

"It could be someone he recognizes," Rit suggested, and when everyone looked at him, he added, "You know, in the picture."

Grace reached over and pulled the sketch Brian had last looked at to the center of the table so everyone could see which one it was. The tormented features of a bound woman made each one glad it was not someone they knew.

Grace voiced what they were all thinking. "Brian must be horrified if he knows who that woman is."

⚜

Brian was mildly surprised by the darkness that greeted him outside the ice cream parlour, but he zeroed in on his important phone call, dialing over and over. Finally his mother's voice answered. He jumped right in. "Mom! Where are you right now?"

"I'm home, Brian. Thank you for the flowers. You sound upset. Is everything all right?" It didn't even cross her mind that an unexplained two-day delay might be upsetting, because it happened frequently. She was sure something more significant had occurred.

"Mom, stay there. Don't go anywhere until I get there. *Please*." He spoke urgently and persuasively.

"Actually, there is someplace I need to go right away, Brian."

"No! Please, just stay until I can speak with you."

"It's been awhile since we've talked, but it surely doesn't merit all of this," she said in a droll tone.

Brian didn't feel like joking around. "Mom, wait for me to get there, okay? Promise me you'll wait! I have something so incredible to tell you, perhaps show you. I know it may change your mind about going on this trip. Give me a chance! Have I ever spoken to you this way before?"

"I do have a call in for a flight, and I need to get a quick visa from a friend in New York."

His mother's independence was also something Brian was used to. "I'll be there in twenty minutes." He closed the phone and, taking a deep breath, rejoined the group inside, but he didn't sit down.

Instead, taking a calming breath, he reached over and touched a corner of the one sketch. "Could I take this with me if I promise to give it back soon?" he asked Bunny gently, searching her eyes for her true response.

She gazed back with childlike sincerity and gave a faint nod of her head.

"Thanks. You don't know what this means to me right now, but I'll explain when I have more time, okay?" When Bunny nodded, Brian turned to the others. "Good night, Greg, Grace. Tomorrow okay for you, Rit ?" At Rit's affirmative, he continued, "I've never had a day like today. Thanks again, Bunny," he said with a smile, and he was gone, his long legs carrying him away at a great pace.

"Wow! I definitely want to hear that explanation." Rit articulated everyone's thoughts this time. Then looking around the small group, he said, "I'm glad I met you guys. Things are jumpin' around here." His lopsided grin made everybody chuckle.

When Grace and Greg turned to each other and started talking animatedly, Rit turned to Bunny and took one of her hands in his without even thinking about it. Then he began to talk in low tones. "I'm glad I met you. You are one special girl. If you need to communicate with someone, I'm your guy." He opened his wallet, took out a card, and handed it to her as he said, "Here's my phone number. If you want to reach me, or especially if you ever need help, call and tap three times loudly into the phone. Then go to the church, and I'll meet you there."

Bunny took a deep breath and let it out slowly, looking back at Rit with an appreciative smile. Nodding her head, she shyly withdrew her hand and began gathering the remaining sketches together.

Then speaking to the whole group, Rit announced, "I also need to leave," and stood up.

"We're going, too," Greg responded. He stood and helped Grace to her feet. Bunny put the pictures in her folder and everyone walked to the register to pay.

"That man who was with you already paid the tab," the waitress informed them when they got there, "tip and all."

"So you just get a big thank you from us," Greg teased her and then slid a couple more dollars across the counter.

The mood always seems good around this guy, Grace thought as they walked out into the cool night air.

"How 'bout I play taxi, since it's so dark?" Greg offered when they reached the sidewalk.

Rit responded, "That's generous, man, and I will accept, since I still haven't picked up any reflectors."

The girls knew they didn't need to answer, so Grace just tucked her arm into Greg's, the younger two copied them amusingly, and down the street they all went, like the troupe that set off for Oz.

13

Violet answered the phone gingerly, tucking it between her ear and shoulder as she dried her dripping wet hands on a nearby towel.

"Hello, Violet speaking."

"Hello, Violet. This is Katherine Sommers. Have you got a moment?"

"Yes, how are you? It's been a very long time!"

"We're fine, so to speak, and I hope you are all doing well. I wondered if I could stop by. I thought it would be an opportune time. You could say that I sniffed out your barbeque."

"How funny! Of course, you're welcome."

"My son, Brian, is already on the guest list, and after something he's shared with me, I feel I must speak with you."

"Yes, I see the connection, and it will be simply wonderful to see *you*! It's a small world."

"Thank you, Violet, I'm glad that it's such a pleasant day for such things."

"Yes, it is. We'll see you soon."

Hanging up, Violet turned to her husband, who was seated at the kitchen table with a cup of coffee steaming in front of him. "Do you remember Senator Sommers's wife?"

"Is that who that was?" he responded, picking up the cup.

"She said she sniffed out our barbeque."

"I wonder what she has on her mind."

"So it makes you wonder too?"

"Of course." Carl Johnson set down the cup in a matter-of-fact way. "A busy woman like that doesn't go around looking for small social events to attend just for entertainment."

Violet nodded in agreement. Smiling appreciatively at him, she stepped over to give him a kiss on top of his head before turning back to the sink, a thoughtful look returning to her face. She contemplated the mysterious phone call while she peeled and diced the boiled potatoes, onions, and hard-cooked eggs for the potato salad she would serve that afternoon, and finally after getting the mayonnaise and mustard out of the refrigerator, she began to put the salad together.

Next, taking one last peek at the baked beans in the oven, she removed her apron and left the kitchen, but as much as she had to do before guests arrived, the intriguing conversation was never far from her mind.

⧎ | ⧎

Grace and Bunny arrived first, Grace having planned to help Violet serve. She discovered Violet's incredible organizational skills when her offer was effectively turned down. Greg's mother had not only finished all the food preparations but also asked members of Greg's young adult fellowship at church to serve punch and replenish the various dishes when necessary.

"Well, since your labor isn't needed," Greg said, grinning at the girls, "why don't we go outside?"

Taking them through the kitchen, Greg escorted Grace and Bunny to the patio, where they could nibble on the snacks already set out while he set up the croquet game on the lawn. There they saw a volleyball net and horseshoes already set up in a corner of the big back yard. As more people started to arrive, the games began, chatter and laughter filling the air and blending with the hickory smoke from the barrel grill, where long slabs of succulent ribs were cooking slowly.

Bunny was absorbed in making a difficult croquet shot when Rit slipped up behind her, placing his hands over her eyes and laughing when she jumped and poked her mallet backward into his ribs. Returning to her shot, she sent the ball straight through the hoop then offered her mallet to Grace, who accepted, saying, "I guess I'll take over your game for you since you're winning."

Greg teased, "Not for long, now that you took over."

They continued their repartee while resuming the play, as Bunny and Rit wandered off in the direction of a small orchard. The next time Grace and Greg looked up, they could see Rit pushing Bunny in an old tire swinging from an apple tree.

"Well, what do you think about that?" Greg asked with a bodyguard-type inflection.

Grace responded softly, "I think it's just fine." She looked up into Greg's eyes, and there was another moment between them that stopped the croquet game—stopped time.

Brian's voice sounded like it came from a different dimension. "What a great day for an outdoor party! This isn't a croquet game; this is a staring contest. Uh-huh, caught you two, and what's going on over there under the old apple tree? Two more lovebirds. Are you sure it's not spring?"

"Well, it's so sunny and mild today that it certainly feels like spring," Grace said, trying to redirect the conversation toward the weather.

Rit helped Bunny out of the swing, and they came across the lawn, bounding playfully along like two lambs.

"You sure are funny, Brian—a real funny guy," Rit called out as they approached. "A late guy, too."

"I've got my reasons," Brian replied, highlighting the mystery in his voice.

"What?" Greg challenged. "Explain to us the great mysteries of life now that we find ourselves all together once again."

As everyone chuckled, Brian said in a more serious tone, "Actually, it does have something to do with living. Now, you would have to know my mother personally for this to have full impact, but…" and Brian proceeded to explain that his mother was the woman in Bunny's drawing and that he had convinced her to slow down enough to look into the phenomenon of the sketch and the vision behind it and, ultimately, to possibly change her plans, which usually seemed etched in stone.

"What relief you must feel," Grace responded, with Bunny nodding emphatically.

"I happen to believe that people have certain gifts from God, and I'm very grateful that there was divine intervention in our lives just now. Look at the world situation. Doesn't this give you hope?" Brian was addressing the whole group, and at his last few words his voice cracked, revealing the emotion behind those words.

Bunny, with uncharacteristic demonstrativeness, ran up and hugged him tightly.

Greg could tell by Brian's stilted words that he probably wasn't used to airing his views about God. Over the last ten years many people had backed away from the organized churches, going for a more private relationship with God, so Brian sharing his thoughts this way was meaningful.

Returning to the role of host, Greg invited Brian to grab a mallet and join the game. But even while the party went on, the matter of God's active presence in people's lives remained on Greg's mind. He genuinely wished everyone on earth would get along with each other and worship God together, but reality indicated that things were moving fast in the opposite direction.

⊰|⊱

During a volleyball game, it occurred to Greg that he hadn't seen his parents circulating for a while. He excused himself from the game to mingle with other groups scattered around the yard and through the house.

He had just touched base with a cluster of people in the living room and had begun to move on when he heard low voices speaking from behind his mother's study door. Then the door opened and his father stepped out into the hallway, saying, "I'd better check the grill." Seeing Greg in the hall, he gave him a rather serious smile and nod, but before he closed the door again, Greg was able to see who it was that remained in the room with his mother. Even though her features were composed at present, he could tell that it was the woman portrayed as one of the captives in Bunny's vision. He suddenly, felt desperate to get away somewhere and pray. *If all the family members of the house disappear, we'll have some bewildered guests,* he thought, so he kept on with his obligations as host, but in his heart, he fervently asked God to protect Brian's mother from doubts that could take her life.

Greg noticed that while most of the people were outside enjoying the colorful fruit dessert, an indistinguishable figure inside the house motioned Brian inside. After a few minutes, Brian came back out and rejoined the party, starting a conversation with a group seated on the patio. Greg decided not to interrupt him despite the rather unusual look he'd had on his face when he came out, but when Brian glanced Greg's way, Greg responded with his most reassuring expression.

⊰ | ⊱

The girls were having an old-fashioned good time. Rit found an effortless way to introduce Bunny to his parents, who had accepted the invitation and found many interesting people to socialize with. Other women had given his mother their business cards so they could stay in touch. His father had won at horseshoes all afternoon and was wearing the biggest smile Rit had seen on his face in a long time. All together, Rit was enjoying an on-top-of-the-world feeling.

When people started leaving, Rit arranged for his family to give Grace and Bunny a ride home. Before leaving, though, Grace located Greg standing by the gate, with his father, saying good-byes. Greg excused himself and, taking her hand, led her to a little herb garden tucked into a sheltered spot on the other side of the house where it would escape at least the first light frosts of the fall.

"I didn't know this was here!" she exclaimed. "How pretty!"

"And tasty," Greg added.

Stooping to pinch a leaf and sniff appreciatively, she added, "Smells fabulous too."

Then they just stood quietly, enjoying the moment. As he stood there, Greg became aware that he'd not let go of Grace's hand and that she hadn't pulled away.

Holding her hand feels so natural, he thought. The picture of his parents still holding hands after all their years together came to mind.

"I love this place," Grace said in hushed tones.

And I love this girl. The thought took Greg by surprise. *How does a guy know if he really loves someone or not? Does it happen so suddenly? How do I turn my brain off for a while?* His thoughts were crowding in on him. *Relax, Greg. Just talk with her.* "I thought you would."

"We're getting a ride home with Rit's family." Grinning, she added, "Apparently Rit has his permit, and my guess is that he wants to impress Bunny with his skills."

Greg interjected, "Are they about ready to go?"

"I think so. I just wanted to thank you…"

Greg wondered if she wasn't trying to give him an opportunity to discuss the more hidden events of the day. "You're so welcome. I want to talk with you some more, but not right now." He was thinking about the situation with Brian's mother. "Do you know that I don't even have your phone number?"

Grace, who had never given her phone number to any boy, rattled the number off so quickly Greg needed to have her repeat it so he could try to remember it. Then they went out the odd little garden gate toward the front yard and, rounding the corner of the house, strolled up behind Rit, Brian, and Bunny, who were standing out on the front walk talking with Rit's parents.

Brian noticed them first. "We seem a little cliquey right now, but I assure you, I met a lot of remarkable people this afternoon. Your parents know some of the same folks mine do. Great barbeque, Greg!" He hesitated, then stepped a little closer to Greg. Pulling him to the side, he began talking with Greg in a low voice.

Rit's mother, a very wise woman, spoke up. "Is everyone riding with us ready to go?"

Grace replied cheerfully, "We're ready whenever you are, Mrs. Han."

"We have the white Chevrolet parked near the corner," Mr. Han informed them, handing Rit the keys. Rit, smiling proudly, led the group down the street.

⚜ | ⚜

Back on the patio, the talk and laughter of her departing guests could still be heard as Violet came up beside her husband and put an affectionate arm around his waist.

"It was a good party, wasn't it, Carl?"

"Yes, everyone seemed to have a really good time. And the food was great!"

Violet grinned and gave Carl a little pat on his stomach. Then breathing a small sigh, she added, "Well, I need to make sure the kids are getting along okay with the clean-up and then give them their money." Picking up a couple of stray napkins on the way, she went inside.

Before long the young helpers trooped out the front door, contribution for their next fellowship event in hand and lots of smiles on their faces. When their voices faded, everything was quiet. Only then could the low murmur of voices be heard coming from Carl's upstairs study. When Violet and Carl retired hours later, the light was still visible under the door.

14

The light was still on in another house too. The different time zones made communications between Katherine Sommers and her friends difficult. This time it was particularly trying. Her friend Meg couldn't be found, nor could several other Americans that had been in the same area.

After Brian's urgent conversation with her, Katherine put her flight plans on hold until she could establish the young artist's credibility with an educator whom she trusted. Now as Katherine methodically dialed the phone, trying number after number, it became apparent to her that the combination of waiting for Brian, their conversation, and then checking out the young artist had probably saved her from also becoming a victim of another international kidnapping.

⊰ | ⊱

Katherine eventually fell asleep with the phone still in her hand, but when it slipped from her grasp and fell to the floor, even that soft thud was enough to wake her. Too on edge to simply go back to sleep, Katherine glanced at her watch and then resumed her investigation.

Finally, having achieved only a verification that four people were missing, she deliberated long and hard before deciding to place one last call.

Just then she heard the main door open and someone start up the stairs. In the central hall, the footsteps paused before coming down the hall toward her room. Then there was a light tap on her door.

"Mother? Are you already up?"

"Brian, are you just coming in?" She was glad he was checking on her. "You may enter." As the door opened, she continued, "Actually, I did and didn't get to bed yet."

Brian knew what she meant; he'd grown up with her diligent and persistent application to any task at hand. She would not quit until she got the job done. "You look upset and determined," he said, inviting her confidence.

Confiding in him wasn't what she was concerned about, however. She supplied him with all the information she'd obtained during the night. Then she told him about the phone call she'd decided to make.

Brian had been quiet, listening carefully, but at this, he reacted. "Not her! She is the nosiest woman in the world! Furthermore, she has poor judgment and can't be trusted!"

"I feel just about the same way, but if anyone could ferret out more information, it would be her."

"She's a loose cannon, Mother. You never know exactly what direction she's going to go with anything you tell her. She has no scruples, no loyalty," he continued to protest.

His mother agreed. "Absolutely true, but tell me, who is better connected to the underground network?"

There was no answer. Brian walked over to her and gently pulled her head against his shoulder. Giving her a tender hug, he said, "Do what you need to do," then wished her good day and started for the door. In the doorway he turned and said with deep emotion, "I'm very thankful that you aren't missing along with Meg and the others."

"I'm grateful too, Brian. I appreciate you and your new friends—and God, who is apparently behind my rescue. It's almost too much to consider."

On the way to his suite, Brian asked the butler to bring his mother some strong hot coffee, aware that she was too preoccupied to make this request herself. He set his television to come on at noon, showered, and then stretched out on his couch. National disasters notwithstanding, he was asleep within seconds.

⚜ | ⚜

Violet, having gotten an excellent night's sleep, also crossed paths with her son. Greg was in the kitchen getting out milk in order to make some cocoa when she entered, planning to begin a batch of bread before she got busy with the rest of her day.

"Good morning," she greeted him quietly as she reached into the cupboard to pull out mixing bowls. "Leave the milk out, please. Better yet, would you heat a couple of cups for me too?"

"Sure, Mom." Greg reached into the stove's pan drawer for a saucepan and poured in a generous amount of milk before turning on the burner. "Are you making bread?"

She nodded. "Thank you, dear."

She sure isn't much of a talker in the morning, Greg reflected as he watched her silently walk over to a cupboard, pull out a packet of yeast, and mix the contents into a small bowl of warm water before starting to get out the rest of her ingredients.

"Brian asked a lot of questions last night."

"Did you know the answers?"

Greg smiled, "No, I didn't, but I gave it a good try."

"If you are just now finished, I'd say that was an exceptionally good try." Violet smiled and tousled his hair as she reached for the milk pan and poured some of the now-warm liquid over the oil, sugar, and salt she'd put into one of the bigger bowls.

Greg took the cocoa mix out of the cupboard and added some to the remaining milk while it finished heating. Then pouring the cocoa into a waiting mug, he sat on a stool and watched his mother mix the rest of her bread ingredients while he sipped his hot drink.

By the time he was done, she had begun to knead the dough. Greg placed his cup in the sink and gave his mother a kiss on the back of her head before he left the kitchen. As he headed back upstairs, Greg thought about how glad he was that he had the parents he did. He knew that everyone's family life was different. Brian, for instance, hardly ever saw his parents.

The all-night conversation had gone to deep levels. Brian was looking for answers, and Greg greatly wished the workings of heaven were simple, but how could the creation even begin to comprehend the Creator? A person would have to make a studied and continued effort even to begin to understand God. And what would the frame of reference be? The only perspective that Greg had ever been able to use was love, and the only time life's hard questions had anything like a reasonable answer for him was when he measured his thoughts against God's love. It was like the level his dad used for carpentry. If his thoughts tilted in a bizarre direction, he could line them up with what he knew about God's character to get them straightened out again. This process didn't "solve the mysteries of the universe" for him, as he had said to Brian, but it kept him grounded.

He showered and crawled between crisp, clean sheets. *Glad it's Saturday*. His thoughts drifted off.

⧉ | ⧉

The smell of fresh bread brought Greg back from a deep sleep. Unaccustomed to sleeping during the day, it took him a moment to be sure what time it was. He was surprised to discover he'd slept for only a few hours. He contemplated calling Brian to see what had transpired regarding his mother's trip to the Middle East. So much had been discussed behind closed doors. He trusted that they had all done their part to stop her, but a person's free will was something even God didn't tamper with. He also knew that his mother wouldn't betray certain confidential things about her student but would probably give counsel only from events that had transpired in the public domain. *Too many unknowns*. Glancing at his clock again, he decided to call Grace first.

⧉ | ⧉

The girls had awakened with a sense of peace and serenity. Even if the whole world was in turmoil, they weren't. Once they were dressed and had taken care of their few Saturday morning chores, they decided it was a perfect day to have a picnic.

Just as they were packing up the sandwiches, chips, and drinks, the phone rang. Grace answered and then placed her hand over the mouthpiece while she excitedly told Bunny, "Guess who!" Bouncing on her toes, she spoke back into the phone, "How are you?"

"I'm feeling like seeing you."

"Well, we packed a little food to take to the park a couple of blocks south of here. Would you like to join us?"

"Would I! Do you have enough?"

"Sure! How many sandwiches can you eat?"

"I'll leave that up to you since I basically invited myself," Greg replied primly and she giggled at his tone when she said her good-bye.

As Grace hung up, Bunny was pulling the lunch meat and bread back out, making faces as if she couldn't quite figure out who the caller was.

"Cute," Grace retorted as she efficiently put together a couple more sandwiches, adding them and another drink to the basket. When Greg pulled up a while later, they were ready to go, anticipating another great day.

⚎|⚏

The sun shown, the dogs barked, and the children played. Grace, Bunny, and Greg played too. They swung on the swings, ate their food, and lay in the shade under a cluster of tall pine trees. They played with a Frisbee and chased each other around the big empty pool and pump house. Bunny seemed an especially free spirit. Running after a cloud of butterflies that had erupted suddenly from a bush they passed, she waved her hands in the air and spun around, trying to get one to land on her finger.

Later Grace watched the setting sun reflect on her sister's peaceful features and thought about how much they'd both changed in just a few weeks. She and Greg sat back down on their blanket, and she leaned against his shoulder, continuing to watch her sister dance off among the elongated shadows of the trees.

Their illusion of well-being carried them as they leisurely gathered their things and slowly returned to the car for the drive home.

⇥|⇤

Ordinarily Greg might not have noticed the dark Town Car parked across the street from the girls' house. It just happened that as they neared the girls' home, a man in a dark suit was crossing the street from the direction of their house and getting into the car, which was parked close to the front of a large rusty van. Something about the man and the odd combination of vehicles got Greg's attention, and he slowed down, asking Grace if she recognized the man or the cars. She shook her head, so Greg sped up a little and drove right past the house.

"What's going on?" Grace inquired lazily. The fresh air and exercise had caused her to become a bit sleepy.

"Probably nothing," Greg replied, but he didn't have a good feeling about what he'd seen. "Your relatives don't have any friends who drive a Lincoln?"

"Not that I know of," she replied, stifling a yawn.

He didn't want to bring them back to the house, but he couldn't think of a single solid reason not to. He drove around the block to stall for time to think.

He'd learned a lot about the girls that day. Throughout the afternoon, the relaxed conversation had produced even the sad story of their mother's death. He understood that the people they lived with, although related, were not close with the girls, and he got a peek at the heartache and loneliness these beautiful young women had endured.

He thought it over. *Leaving them relatively unprotected...makes me feel uneasy.* Then he decided. "How would you ladies like to come to church with us tomorrow?" He decided the idea was inspired. "In fact, let's just spend the weekend together. Come on, we can pick up some overnight things at your place and go back to my house right now."

The girls looked at him in surprise.

"My folks would love to have you stay. And in the morning, we can all walk to church together." He spoke coaxingly as he parked in front of the house one door past theirs.

Grace tipped her head with a doubtful expression and her hand on the car door. "We just accepted your parents' hospitality yesterday, Greg. We don't want to intrude."

"And I accepted your invitation today. Now it's my turn again." Greg grinned, knowing he'd scored the winning argument.

Bunny clapped her hands together lightly in a pleased manner, and Grace laughed. "Do you always get your way? Bunny, I can collect our things." She hopped out of the car. "I'll be right back."

Greg had not wanted to look back until at least one girl was out of the car. Now he turned around. Looking past Bunny, who was gazing after her sister, he quickly checked to see if the car was still there. It was. Worse yet, the driver had gotten out of the car again and was walking in their direction. Greg put his car in gear and drove around the block again, slowly. *If only there was street access to that back door they use so often*, he urgently wished.

When he approached the house once more, Grace was coming out and just closing the front door behind her. He stopped right in line with her front walk, and she had barely shut the car door when he took off again. A glance in the rear view mirror showed him that the driver, who had returned to the car again, and this time the passenger as well, were half out of the car looking after them.

Greg could tell by the sisters' carefree attitude that they had no expectations and no curiosity about those professional-looking visitors. Greg concluded that men react to situations much differently than women and almost started minimizing the incident until he happened to glance in the side mirror as he changed lanes and spotted the Lincoln again. It was two cars behind them, and as he watched, he saw that it changed lanes when he did. Without comment, he got on the freeway as soon as he could and increased his speed gradually.

Grace was leaning back with her eyes closed, but Greg noticed Bunny leaning forward with question marks in her eyes. "I don't usually go this way, but I thought I'd stop at the store and pick up some things. That okay?" She nodded her head and relaxed into the back seat. *Good, neither one has noticed the car following us*, he noted while he formulated a plan.

He slowed down just enough that the driver between them and the town car grew impatient and passed them. With the town car now right on their tail, Greg kept up his speed until he had almost passed his exit. Then he abruptly turned without signaling, barely making the exit ramp. Unprepared, the other driver went on past it. The maneuver brought Grace suddenly upright, a startled look on her face. "Oops, I almost didn't make my turn," was all he said. *That much was definitely true*, he said to himself. He resolved to speak with his dad about the situation at first opportunity.

Greg took a circuitous route back the way they'd come, using less-traveled streets where he could and checking periodically to make sure the men in the Lincoln had not picked them up again. Satisfied that they hadn't, he stopped at a quick-shop, where he called home to let them know he was bringing house guests and then bought hot deli chicken baskets, sodas, and snacks, as well as orange juice and a big box of doughnuts for breakfast. He quickly returned to the car, theorizing that staying in motion was a better way not to be found. He passed out chicken baskets and napkins then drove on side streets all the way home.

Violet made the girls entirely comfortable upon their arrival, putting fresh linens in the guest rooms then serving tea and the snacks Greg had bought. Carl built a crackling fire in the big living room fireplace, and Violet started a game of Scrabble with Grace and Bunny. They were so entertained and cozy that they hardly noticed Greg and his father slip out of the room to talk. When the men returned, they each had a serious look, but nothing in their demeanor was alarming or made the women feel insecure.

Greg gave Grace a light kiss on the forehead when all of them were saying good night. He softly pulled one of Bunny's curls, saying, "*Boing!*" She grinned, and wiggling her fingers at everyone, headed up the stairs toward the room made up for her with Grace right behind her.

When the girls were out of earshot, Greg looked hesitantly from his dad to his mom. "I'll fill her in, son," Carl reassured him. "I'm proud of you. Sleep well."

"You too, Dad, Mom," Greg said. Then he too headed up the stairs.

Once he was in bed, Greg remembered the connection with Brian's situation that he'd wanted to make earlier. *There are so many different things going on*, he thought, *or are they different things?*

15

The phone call was made and there was no taking it back. Brian's mother had an increasingly uneasy feeling throughout the conversation, but she deemed the seriousness of the situation to need the measures she took. The reporter seemed elated and eager to dig into the story, but her questioning leaned more toward Bunny's phenomenally accurate vision than finding out about the people who were probably now hostages.

When the phone was back in its cradle, Brian's mother sat staring into space, as if she were trying to view the results of her call. She didn't hear the geese honking as they flew overhead on their way south or the neighbor's dog barking at the geese. After several hours, she didn't even hear the phone ringing because she'd fallen asleep again, the deep slumber of one depleted.

⇥ | ⇤

Brian got to the phone on the last ring. The man calling first asked for Brian's mother, but when Brian said she wasn't available, the man proceeded to question him about Bunny, the vision, and where she lived. Brian became irritated, stating that he had no information to give until he finally just said good-bye and started to hang up. Before the phone clicked off, however, he heard the man address someone else, saying, "We'll just go online to find out—"

After hanging up, Brian paced back and forth across the foyer several times. Unable to calm himself, he took his keys out of his pocket unconsciously and stood jingling them as he stared out a front window until his agitation forced him out of the house. Trotting around the house to the garage without a plan, he backed his car out and drove off in a whirl of leaves.

Driving usually helped Brian sort things out, but this afternoon this practice didn't help right away. For a while he tried thinking of pleasant things instead of problems to regain his perspective. The party at Greg's house came to mind, and following this trend, he considered Rit's parents. They were so humble and soft-spoken. Most families Brian knew would have told and retold the story of how their son had saved them from a drive-by shooting in the middle of the night, and truly it was a story worth telling. But these quiet people hadn't drawn any attention to themselves, only blending in, obviously enjoying the social chatter and games. They accepted Bunny with intuitive grace and treated Brian like an old friend of the family.

As he reflected on the results of learning and experience, the other things he pondered finally resulted in a plan. He made two calls on his cell phone and then turned on the radio, which helped him begin to relax.

His relaxation, however, was cut short by the news broadcast. "…four American hostages being held somewhere in that region. We'll know more when the group responsible makes their demands…" He pushed the radio's off button. *Mother was right; that reporter didn't waste any time.*

His thoughts went back on their despondent journey. That reporter seemed to have tentacles that reached in every direction. He could sense them stretching out toward little Bunny as the darkness deepened that evening. *Information, ratings, fame, greed.*

Brian pulled up in front of Rit's house. He was an information gatherer by nature, but in the last twenty-four hours, he'd developed even more into a seeker of truth.

Rit's mother opened the screen door for him. "Come in, Brian. Thank you for calling with such a wonderful idea. We like that place."

He followed her into the living room. "It's one of our family's favorites, Mrs. Han. I should be honest, though. I didn't just do this for you." She waited him out with a patient smile on her face. "I need to talk with Mr. Han, if he has some time this evening." Brian had determined that Mr. Han was a wise man to have brought his family so far in a strange, new country. He had a hunch that Mr. Han may have valuable insight. *Am I having more of these intuitions lately, than ever before*, he mused as he glanced up at the sound of an approaching voice.

"I have time," answered the older man, stepping out of his study and stretching out his hand toward Brian, who shook it gratefully. Just then a van slowly drove by and then stopped, backed up, and parked in front of Brian's car. A wonderful aroma wafted toward them as Brian held open the front door for the men carrying in their big covered trays.

"Dinner is served," Brian said with a comical flourish of his hand.

"You like to do that," said Rit, who had just come into the room also. Then he copied Brian, so that both of them ended up standing at the door like a welcoming committee for the people bringing in food.

Everyone was in a good mood as they sat down to dinner. Conversation flowed easily, and Mrs. Han, stretching out her feet in a contented way under the table, particularly enjoyed being served a feast in her own home. The table talk continued until the caterers had done the clean-up and whisked all of their dishes and pans back out the door. Rit's mother, her face wreathed in smiles, thanked Brian and excused herself for the evening.

Rit was left trying to discern whether or not he should leave too, having overheard Brian's request for his father's time. But when his father suggested that they adjourn to his study, he included Rit in his sweeping gesture, so with a quick glance at Brian, who seemed amenable, Rit accompanied them to the comfortable chairs in his father's private study.

Hot tea awaited them on his father's big desk. *How does she get things done so well?* Rit thought appreciatively of his mother. By the end of the evening, he also admired his father even more.

Mr. Han picked up the thread of small talk for a few minutes. He courteously inquired about Brian's family, their whereabouts, and their health. Soon, however, Brian cut to the chase.

"Mr. Han, my mother's trip to help a friend of hers has been miraculously stopped by a series of supernatural events." Brian tried to explain succinctly, bringing Mr. Han up to date. Mr. Han leaned forward in his chair with his eyes fixed on Brian throughout the telling, except for a quick look at Rit when Brian got to the part where the family's near disaster had been predicted in Bunny's drawing the day before it happened.

Brian ended his tale by recapitulating the news report, and Mr. Han finally spoke, commenting, "I was listening to that report right before you arrived, Brian." There was a long pause as Mr. Han brought his folded hands to his face, pressing his two index fingers on the bridge of his nose in thought. Then straightening up in the chair, he began, speaking slowly and carefully choosing his words.

"My family escaped from China after the change of power. It was very difficult, but my father was able to stay military in Taiwan. It was not an easy life. My father could seldom be at home. My mother was alone in Taipei most of the time, struggling to raise my brothers, sisters, and me. We were able to survive, but we felt life would be better in America if we could get here. So we kept trying until we were able to get to the United States.

"These years have sometimes been challenging, but it is good here. My wife and I are thankful, and here we have hope. The American system is much better than many other places. We have chosen well. Right now, terrorists and greedy men in power upset the world. We have to stick together, work together. We have to listen to each other and protect each other in our daily lives."

Brian and Rit glanced at each other and then looked back at Mr. Han, wondering what he was going to say next. He sat silently, as if he were waiting.

Brian let Mr. Han's words sink in some more, and then he realized his questions had been addressed. If a situation developed closer to home, this family was willing to network for a solution. Brian wanted to hug Mr. Han, but his upbringing wouldn't permit such an exhibition. Instead he nodded, beaming, and slapped Rit on the back a couple times.

Rit responded with a suggestion that Brian stay in the guest room, which was agreeable with everyone, and the men drank their tea together while Mr. Han gave a few more narratives in response to Brian's inquiries about how they had reached America. None of them knew what tomorrow would bring as they said their good nights, but each of the three men sensed there was a growing peril headed toward their families, like lava from a volcanic eruption—quiet, dangerous, and unstoppable.

16

Morning brought crisp fall weather. The sun shone, but the air was getting cooler.

"A front is coming in," Violet remarked at breakfast, which was quick and easy. Doughnuts, orange juice, and coffee, and they were off to church.

The girls had an unexpectedly wonderful time. During their walk to the church, Grace had admitted to having a preconceived idea about Christian worship services. She told Greg honestly that she thought they would feel they didn't belong there, that it would be intimidating and maybe boring.

"Why don't you tell me what you really think?" was Greg's dry comment.

Bunny looked a little concerned that they might have offended, but Grace, who had decided to voice the fears they'd already discussed in their own unique way, very much trusted Greg's and his parents' ability to deal with truthfulness. The Johnson family didn't disappoint the girls. Violet gave Grace a little hug. Carl Johnson said, "If you feel uncomfortable, just let one of us know, and we'll get you out of there." Greg just wiggled his eyebrows up and down twice with a grin.

The girls first discovered that church was a big social place where people connected, enjoying conversation and catching up with each other's busy lives. Then they found that the worship part was deeply meaningful. The songs celebrated God's greatness and power, voiced thankfulness for sustenance and goodness in life, rejoiced over forgiveness and a fresh start, or asked for help through hard times, pledging love and allegiance to their Savior. The sermon was relevant to current events and explained how sin makes the world wretched and evil, but how this can be changed by letting God work with one's heart. The pastor assured everyone that God has a loving plan for their lives, just like a good father, who knows his children's strong points, develops goals for them, and supports their efforts toward those goals one hundred percent.

Afterward, while the older people went to the fellowship hall for the coffee hour, Greg took the girls to the young people's center and introduced them to all of his friends, pointing out the ones who'd been at the barbeque and giving whispered reminders of names. Somehow even Bunny felt included in the general chatter and amusements. The young people had a whole section of the church building to call their own, with billiards and ping-pong tables, a gym with a full-sized basketball court, a mini theater, and a small kitchen. It was like a community center where just about everyone was on the same pleasant page.

As they all walked back to the Johnsons' home, Grace remarked on the complete lack of pressure she had felt from the people she'd met. "I felt like I could just be myself," she confided shyly to Greg. He was about to give a supportive response when the whole family stopped on the sidewalk a block from the house.

"What do they think they're doing?" Greg's dad quickly pulled out his cell phone and placed a call to his old precinct station. "Carl Johnson here. Could you send a couple cars out to my place right away? Thanks." He snapped the phone shut then turned to Violet, a grim look on his face. "Honey, why don't you take the girls the back way?"

Violet just nodded, understanding his message, and taking Grace and Bunny by the hand, led them around the corner and toward the alley that ran behind the Johnsons' property. Carl continued toward their house, moving down the sidewalk with a determined stride, Greg at his side.

Violet smiled reassuringly at the girls, who were beginning to look alarmed. "Wait until you see how we get in. I'm so glad we have this option now. We've joked around about having a secret escape route, but I never thought I'd have to use it to get *into* the house."

Violet was chirping like a bright songbird on a sunny day, and the girls, though their questions showed on their faces, went with her trustingly. Reaching the back edge of the Johnsons' lot, the three entered a garden shed right off the alley. Once they were inside the damp-earth-smelling structure, Violet carefully closed the door and then began moving aside some empty boxes stacked to one side. The girls saw that beneath them was a trap door, its handle a big iron ring. When Violet pulled it open, an even mustier, narrow staircase was disclosed.

"Careful. It's slippery," she warned as she motioned for them to go ahead of her. Violet reached in and switched on a light, then pulled the door shut as she came down too.

Turning at the bottom of the steps into a low-ceilinged tunnel, they soon reached another, shorter set of steps, these leading up to a low, old-fashioned plank door. Once Violet had opened it with the large key she retrieved from a dark crack between the wall and the ceiling near the top of the door, even Bunny had to duck her head to keep from hitting it on the frame as they entered a storeroom lined with shelves of fruit, relishes, and preserves in canning jars. This room, in turn, opened into the basement of the house. Violet took a moment to replace the key. Then after carefully locking the door again, using an identical key retrieved from a similar crack above the storeroom door, she led the girls upstairs.

The feeling of strangeness increased as Violet and Grace peeked through the curtains when they got to one of the guest rooms. The window faced the street, and they could see that the whole yard was filled with reporters, huge cameras, mobile light fixtures, make-up people, and men with dark suits and ties that looked like government agents. Then they saw lights flashing on squad cars that were coming into the neighborhood without sirens. When Bunny ducked under Grace's elbow to take a look for herself, she suddenly fainted.

Grace was shocked, feeling rather nauseated as well, but when her sister fell to the floor, she forgot her own distress and knelt on the floorboards, fanning the air around Bunny's face, calling her name repeatedly. Violet knelt beside her, helping her disoriented pupil sit up slowly as her consciousness returned. Grace attempted to explain why Bunny might have reacted this way, but

Violet assured her that she didn't need to know right then, and together they made Bunny comfortable on the nearby bed, fixing the pillows for her and placing a satin coverlet over her knees.

Violet excused herself to get the lemonade she felt would refresh them as Greg appeared and asked to speak with Grace privately for a few moments.

Grace looked questioningly at her sister. "Will you be okay?" she asked solicitously. Bunny nodded without taking her eyes from the curtained window. "I think she'll be all right," Grace told Greg as she joined him in the hallway, but her tone was doubtful.

"Let's borrow my dad's study for a few minutes," Greg suggested, and he led the way down the hall, opening the door while stepping aside to let her enter. Grace sat down in the big leather chair near the window, and Greg perched on the side of the desk.

"I took the liberty of calling your relatives," he told her. "When I asked how things were over there, they said they'd had visitors late yesterday afternoon. Today they've had reporters calling and driving around their neighborhood, but none have stopped and parked themselves on the lawn like they have here." When he mentioned those visitors, he thought of the car that had followed them the day before, but he avoided mentioning it to Grace.

"How did they ever find out we were here?" Grace wondered.

"I think they searched online for any connections Bunny had. Academic records would have shown my mother as her supervisor. Hopefully, my dad will run them off, but we need to find a place for you to wait out this storm."

As they discussed serious considerations, they had no clue that Bunny was taking matters into her own hands. She'd used the guest room phone to call Rit's number, and when his dad answered, she tapped three times plainly and hung up. She waited a few minutes then dialed the same number again. This time Rit answered with much concern in just his hello. She repeated the three distinct taps, and hanging up again, she went quickly into the next room, where her things were in the bag Grace had packed. She retrieved her folder from the bottom of the bag where her sister had carefully placed it, and slipping like a shadow back down all the stairs, she went out the tunnel to the alley.

⚜ | ⚜

Scurrying down a different combination of streets to the church, Bunny managed to get inside safely undiscovered. There she found her way to the choir loft and sat down with her heart pounding. She wished she'd been able to secure the sketch Brian had borrowed because she was pretty sure that it was that particular sketch that brought all of this upon them.

It was so quiet in the sanctuary that she heard the footsteps before she saw anyone. She dropped to her knees and peeked over the railing. Her rapid breathing seemed too loud, and she tried to breathe in and out more slowly, her condensing breath moistening the wooden rail that she gripped so tightly. She then saw who it was. Rit was walking slowly down the aisle, bending in an odd way because as he passed every pew, he stooped to peer underneath. Bunny put her head down on the rail as her fingers slipped off, her tears blending with the existing dampness, and she felt unable to let him know exactly where she was.

She heard steps on the carpeted stairs to the loft and was about to stand up when the person near the top spoke. "I know I saw someone come in here." The voice was deep and businesslike. Bunny lay down and rolled under the pew, shaking furiously.

That was how Rit found her a few minutes later, after he had distracted the two men in black suits that were checking out the church. They hadn't given away their objective, though, as Rit showed up near the bottom of the loft stairs. He backed slowly away from them, pretending he didn't speak English and talking glibly in Chinese until they gave up asking him questions and left the building.

When he at last found her, Rit tried to help Bunny up, but she just scooted even farther under the bench. By the way she was shaking, Rit worried that she might even be going into shock. Looking around for a warm covering of some kind, all he could see anywhere in the large sanctuary was the altar cloth, so he ran down the stairs and to the front of the church. Closing his eyes, he talked to God in his heart. *Jesus, you know I don't mean any disrespect, and you know why I need this, okay? Thanks.* He pulled the cloth from under the few things sitting on it and ran back up the stairs. After he had stuffed the cloth around her as best he could, he ran back down again to find Brian.

Brian had offered a ride as soon as Rit had given half an explanation, which he completed in the car on the way, but when Rit looked outside now for the Mercedes, it wasn't where he thought it would be. The lonely, empty feeling he'd felt the night of his family's recent crisis resurfaced. He was willing to help but felt so helpless. *The situation is too big for me, for anybody.* Rit felt dejected watching this incident circling outward like ripples in water, farther into the world's current tormented series of events. *I wish sometimes that I couldn't figure things out. Then you give me dreams too.* He became conscious he was talking to God again, and he realized something else: the empty confusion was gone. His thoughts quickly went on. *Now, if I was speaking to a wall, I'm sure I wouldn't feel gratified, so therefore I'm aware of a connection with another living soul. I'm sorry it's taken me so long to acknowledge you. Your existence was vague to me until this moment. Even when I asked you about the altar cloth, it was mostly a precaution, but somehow, right now, I'm positive you're my friend and that you'll help us.*

Brian walked up at that instant. "Did you find her? You look different, calm. You must have found her. Where is she?"

"Actually, she's up those stairs under a bench, and she was shaking like a half-frozen kitten, so I came down to find you." They hurried up the stairs as Rit continued, "Did you see those big dudes in suits?"

"Yes. That's why I moved the car."

As they reached the front of the choir loft, Brian spotted Bunny under the seat. "Oh, Bunny! Here, let us help you out from under there." Brain bent down, first pulling the altar cloth out. He spread it on the floor. Then he gently pulled Bunny out and rolled her onto the cloth. He wrapped it snugly around her and her folder as he said, "Great blanket," glancing at Rit.

"It was all I could find. *He* didn't mind," Rit said with a nod toward the cross behind the altar.

Brian started to chuckle, gave Rit a strange look, and then just scooped Bunny up in his arms and headed for the stairs. "Follow me."

Rit was right behind him. "What are we going to do with her?"

A muffled reply came from the back seat as Brian laid his burden down carefully. Then standing back up, he said, "I have no idea," frowning a bit as he looked thoughtfully at the ashen-faced girl huddled on the back seat wrapped in an altar cloth.

17

They searched the house, the tunnel, the back yard, and even down the alley. Grace had discovered that Bunny's folder was missing as well. As they were in the midst of their search, Carl found two bugs in the house, so as the search went on, he had to include debugging as well. He warned the others not to discuss any private matters. He also called his old chief down at the precinct station and the local FBI office to protest the invasion of his family's privacy, but he carefully avoided conversation with any of the reporters outside. Some had drifted away during the afternoon, but there were still others persistently trying to get a statement from anyone in the house.

Violet took a few moments from the quest to make sandwiches and change clothes. While she was in her room, the phone rang. When she answered, there was a brief silence, and then a young man's voice asked, with the slightest accent, "Violet?" With relief she recognized the caller.

"Hello, Rit !" She went on immediately with caution in her voice. "Rit, we have a strange situation here, and I cannot discuss anything right now. Do you understand?"

There was a lengthy pause. Rit heard the strange emphasis on her words *cannot discuss*, and he wasn't sure what to say. But thinking of all that had been going on—the reactions from Bunny and the questions he and Brian had been asking, he decided to play to the worst-case scenario. "I just wanted to thank you for the fun party the other day."

"Oh, you're entirely welcome, Rit. It was the best party ever, and your whole family was there, except your sister was missing. Have you seen her?"

Quickly picking up on her clues, Rit smoothly replied, "Yes, as a matter-of-fact, she is over here now. She said she forgot it was the day for the party and was at her boyfriend's house. I'm supposed to convey her apology. She hopes that you are not offended that she didn't attend."

"No, no, of course not. I understand." Violet worked to keep the relief she felt out of her voice. "Tell her we'll see her next time, and please greet your dear parents for us too."

"I sure will. " Rit wrapped it up quickly. "Well, I'd better go. Bye, Violet."

⇥|⇤

When he had hung up, he turned to Bunny and Brian. "There are either taps on the phone or bugs in the house or someone was standing right there listening. Whatever it was, she didn't want to talk about Bunny just then. Should we take her home?"

Bunny shook her head no and started trembling slightly again.

Brian looked pensive for a moment and then made a decision. "Let's get her to my place."

"But they know that your family is involved. They don't know anything about me."

"Even though you were discreet, they do have your number if they're tracing calls. I think they'd be less likely to actively hassle a senator's family," Brian insisted, hoping that was true. "Besides, we have a lot of unoccupied rooms and staff to watch over her during the day."

❧ | ❧

Violet tried to get everyone together in the kitchen to give them the news she'd learned even though she realized that she'd have to be very cautious about how she did it.

The quiet meeting she envisioned didn't happen, however, because Carl was now irate. Storming into the room, he told her, "Now I've found a camera, and I don't know how many others there might be or where they're placed! They must actually have come in here while we were at church, and who knows what they've done. We might as well move; we have no more privacy!"

"Calm down, honey." Violet placed a hand on his shoulder, but he quickly shook it off. Instead he stalked over to the kitchen sink, and resting stiff arms on the ceramic, he glared out the window at the reporters that were now in the backyard too.

Violet glanced at Greg, who grimaced and then whispered to Grace, "My dad hardly ever gets so upset, but when he does…"

Then Violet, a possible solution coming to mind, spoke up in a bright voice. "Why don't we go for a little drive—a break for all of us? In fact, maybe Bunny went out for a walk, and we'll see her if we drive around."

Seeing Carl turn and look at her, studying her face for a moment, Violet thought that he might have caught the slight inflection in her voice. *Being married for a really long time has its merits,* she thought.

"Maybe later," he said, and he waved for them to follow him to the garage. A reporter who spotted them was warned off at least briefly by a fierce glare from the big, broad-shouldered man.

When he opened the garage door, Carl glanced around. Everything looked orderly, the way it ordinarily did. Then his eyes lit on a bag of grass seed he'd picked up the last time he was out, now on the floor next to the Jeep. With a determined set to his jaw, he motioned for everyone to get into the car but put his finger to his lips, warning them to watch what they said, even here.

When everyone was in the car, Carl quickly backed down the driveway and sped down the street. He shed those who tried to follow with several minutes of the evasive maneuvers years of police work had taught him. Soon they were well away from their part of town. Carl pulled over once, briefly, onto the shoulder of the road to remove something from underneath the Jeep and toss it into a nearby pond before continuing on. Though a few questioning looks were cast Carl's way, the others just chatted about church, school, and the weather as the big man drove on.

About twenty minutes later, he abruptly pulled into the lot of a car rental place, parked, and got out of the car, saying nothing but giving them all one more warning look. He then went inside. Soon he came out carrying a set of keys and motioned them toward a big, silver SUV parked nearby.

As they drove away in the new vehicle, there was a barrage of questions. Violet waited until everyone had aired the queries, and then she said, "Bunny is at Rit's house," and before her husband could fret about the insecure phone line, she added, "We didn't actually say anything about her, and I'm really not sure how she got there, but I'm sure she's there."

"Okay. Good. Now we'll all move to Florida." Carl spoke like a statue, staring straight ahead. The comment was humorous, but, at the same time, not funny at all. Their lives had changed and would never be the same. If everything went back to the way it was before church that morning, they would still have new suspicions and doubts about their privacy and way of life. Their peaceful existence had been ripped away from them, never to be completely recovered again.

The foursome discussed whether or not they should try to call Rit's house. Grace was anxious to make contact with her sister and wanted her to have a voice in any decisions made. A drive-up payphone seemed to be the instrument to look for, and they kept driving and looking until they found one.

Carl pulled up to it in a position that allowed Grace to take the receiver into her window. Violet looked up the number in the address book she carried in her purse, and Grace leaned out to dial. The phone rang several times until Mrs. Han answered a little breathlessly and told Grace that the guys had taken Bunny somewhere else and that, no, she wasn't sure where. Grace thanked her, hanging up with a big sigh. Leaving her arms draped over the edge of the window, she laid her head down between them.

Greg put his hand on her back and peeked underneath to see her face. There were tears on her cheeks, so he gathered her up in his arms while Violet invited her to stay with them until the whole thing blew over.

"Knowing the media, they will move on to something new and different—maybe tomorrow," she said.

"We're forgetting the suits," Carl objected. "When those guys come around, there is more going on than the usual daily news. I don't even want to go back home right now." Thinking just a moment, he then went on in a voice of kind authority. "How would you all like it if I treat us to a few days at a hotel? You gals can shop, and we guys will use the spa."

"That is a good suggestion, dear." Violet smiled broadly, turning to the others. "Would you like that Grace? Greg? We can continue trying to contact Bunny from a more secure place."

Grace sat up, wiping her face with the back of her hand, her expression lightening a bit as she looked appreciatively at Violet and Carl. "That idea makes me feel better. I didn't want to go…home. Thank you so much." She thought for a few minutes and spoke again with a note of concern in her voice. "Maybe you should take me home, though. If you went back to your house without my sister or me, the press would probably leave you alone after a few questions."

"I don't want to be asked even one more question," Carl responded with gruff humor. "We're here for you, Gracie. You just relax. I know Greg doesn't mind."

Grace took a quick look at Greg, a soft, brief smile and a slight blush coming to her face. Then she leaned her head back against the seat and relaxed, gazing quietly out the window.

⊰ | ⊱

After a good dinner in the hotel restaurant, the women went shopping, promising to leave the newly purchased swim trunks at the lobby desk and meet the men poolside later. Violet enjoyed having a chance to get to know Grace better. People's most interesting characteristics seemed to emerge during adversities, and Grace was holding up very well, in Violet's estimation. After shopping, they each went to their own room to change before rejoining the men down by the indoor pool.

⊰ | ⊱

Grace had never had much of a mother, yet the warmth of Violet's approval reminded her of the few times her mother had read a bedtime story or made breakfast before school. She looked with satisfaction at her new swimsuit in the dresser mirror and then slipped on the tunic that went with it. After fastening her hair back in a ponytail, she put the room keycard into her pocket and left for the pool. Stepping lightly down the hall, she chose the stairs instead of using the elevator.

Meeting in the hallway downstairs, the two women made an entrance together. Once inside, they took off their outer tunics and placed them on lounge chairs next to the pool and turned to greet Carl and Greg in their new swim wear, to which the men showed appropriate approval. Then sidling up next to them with a wink at each other, the men gave both women a little push into the deep end of the pool.

Grace started splashing and sputtering. "I can't swim! I can't swim!" she cried, luring Greg to dive in to save her, but when he got close enough to help, she suddenly swam under water to the opposite edge of the pool and came up laughing. Greg treaded water in the middle of the pool while listening to his mother reprimand his dad. "Did you read that sign, officer? It says No Horseplay." His dad hung his head in mock shame.

"I think the joke's on us, Dad," Greg jested.

"Always is, son. Always is," his dad replied, getting a laugh from some other men that were swimming and sitting in chairs around the pool.

Greg swam over to Grace, who splashed him playfully. The parents relocated to the Jacuzzi at the far end of the room and later slipped up to their room without disturbing the young people's rapport. Indeed, two hours passed before Grace looked around to see where the older couple was and, finding them gone, suggested that she and Greg follow their example.

Greg admitted that he didn't want the evening to end, but he conceded that it might be good to call it a day if they were to get an early start in the morning, and he walked Grace to her room. He hesitated at her door. *It sure would be easy to take advantage of her emotional vulnerability right now, wouldn't it, Greg?* he thought, but a lifetime of training held, and he only said, "You make me totally forget about time, Grace. I even forgot our troubles for the evening." Drawing her into his arms, he held her close for a long moment before pulling back to look at her for another long moment. *I'm so tempted!* "Sleep well, Grace. See you in the morning." He dropped his hands to his side and turned to walk away, battle won.

"You too, Greg," Grace called over her shoulder as she inserted the card into the slot on the door.

Carl spoke softly in the dark. "Violet, you awake?"

"Yes," she replied, her voice revealing that she too had simply been lying there thinking. "Do you suppose there's any reason why we should wait until morning to find Grace's sister?" he inquired.

18

Bunny rode with Rit sitting beside her in the back seat, Brian driving them like a chauffeur. Rit had received his father's permission to take two days off school, an astonishing concession considering how Mr. Han felt about education, and now they were taking Bunny to Brian's stately dwelling.

Though at first they had considered putting her in the Sommerses' guesthouse, they finally concluded the mansion itself was better. When they arrived, the two young men got Bunny out of the car and walked her inside. Guiding her down the hallway, Brian led her to a guestroom that had its own bath and little sitting area.

"You should be perfectly safe as long as you're in here, even if we're not around." Showing her around, Brian pointed out the locks on doors and windows first and then showed her the intercom phone. "Here, just push this button after you pick up the receiver, and someone will come to find out what you need. Just use the paper by the outside phone over there by your bed to write down any requests." Then guiding her around the room, he told her, "There's the bathroom; it's all set with towels and shampoo and any other stuff you're likely to need, and here's the closet." Opening the door to show her, he added, "One of these bathrobes and a pair of these slippers ought to work for you."

There was nothing lacking for her comfort. Watching for a response on her part, the young men saw her eyes fill with tears, and not knowing how to interpret her tears, they both leaned toward her, their eyes showing immediate concern.

Their reaction made her smile through her tears, and going to the phone, she picked up the little pad of paper and pen next to it and wrote *I'm so grateful. Thank you.*

"Whew!" Rit sighed with relief. "I thought you were going to hate it or something. I thought you were going to need your favorite teddy bear to be able to sleep." Bunny swatted at him in a good-natured manner, and he jumped back with a laugh, making her miss.

"I'll let you kids play," Brian said lightly. "Rit, you know the ropes, so enjoy yourselves while I check into a few things. All right?"

"Got it. Thanks, man." Rit felt like a lemon situation was turning into lemonade, and he asked Bunny, "Do you like to read?"

"There you go," Brian said with approval, knowing where Rit was headed. "If you two will excuse me, please?" He went back toward the front staircase while Rit took Bunny by the hand, leading her to the library just a little farther down the hallway.

⋈

Brian found his mother in her darkened sitting room, leaning back in a big chair with a cool cloth on her forehead, feet propped up on her antique footstool.

"Mother?"

"Brian. I have rarely made such a grave mistake as the one I made in the last day or so."

"Mother—"

"No, let me finish, son. The call I made has had irreversible consequences. And one of them is the migraine I've had ever since." She moaned, rubbing her temples in a circular motion. "Although Meg's disappearance got quicker attention from the State Department, the press is avidly trying to explore the supernatural aspect of this situation."

"Mother, I know. It's okay, though. The girl is here."

"Here? She's here under our roof? I'm not sure that's good, Brian. The reporters have been asking a lot of questions. A special agent has been here as well."

"Did you speak with any of them, or did you decline comment?"

"I declined. In fact, I sent down excuses to the agent as well."

"So you believe they'll be back."

"Yes, I do." There was a long pause. "Could I meet her, Brian? I'm ashamed that I brought her such trouble after she virtually saved my life—she along with your evaluation and loving persistence—but my gratitude overrides my embarrassment."

"I don't think she'll hold your decision against you. You had a friend in trouble, and something had to be done, but there's something else to consider. Have you wondered why she drew the scene?"

"I thought perhaps she is a psychic artist?"

Brian smiled at the picture that came to mind, so unlike Bunny. "She's not that," he replied. "She is mute." There was another long pause.

She moaned again, but this time it was not because of her headache, "You're not telling me she's vocally impaired, son. Please don't tell me I've managed to get a little disabled girl into all this trouble."

"Mother, I'll share this burden with you. I'm not in the habit of disclosing people's confidential problems, and I didn't reveal much about the artist when I was trying to convince you to cancel your plans to go to Meg's aid, but I see now that if I had told you more about Bunny, it might have tipped the scales in favor of not calling that particular reporter."

"Hind sight is the best sight," she said flatly.

She must be extremely fatigued, Brian thought, knowing how his mother usually avoided the use of old sayings. He said comfortingly, "We'll get through this. Our family knows how to deal with the press, and you will rise to the occasion, I'm sure. Let me arrange for dinner to be served in the dining room, and I'll have Bunny seated next to you. Our friend Rit is here too."

"Very good, Brian. Could you bring her to my study first, though, maybe ten minutes before dinner?" Her request was actually a polite command.

He nodded, and picking up her hand, he gave it a gentle squeeze. "See? That's the mother I know and love."

⇥|⇤

Brian found both Rit and Bunny in the library, their respective noses in books. *How well suited they are. If only she could speak her thoughts.* The two readers didn't even notice his entrance until he spoke. "Hello. Would you two care to join us for dinner in about an hour?"

Bunny and Rit looked up, only gradually returning to the present from whatever they had been reading. They exchanged an unspoken question to each other; then Rit responded, "Sure, Brian. Who's us? Is your mother home? I would love to meet her!" Bunny nodded her agreement with Rit.

"Yes, and she'd like to speak with you privately, Bunny, a few minutes before dinner—nothing against you, Rit." Brian grinned at his young study partner and then excused himself again.

Brian cogitated on Bunny's well-being. *Actually, they get on very well with Bunny just the way she is.* Now that she was under his roof, he was feeling a deeper responsibility for helping her in any way he could. He kept this train of thought all the way to the manager's office. *I could talk to her about seeing our family's physician, or maybe a psychologist. One of them might be able to help her regain her speech.*

He had arrived at his destination, and Jim Stevens, who served as both house manager and butler, was looking up at him questioningly from behind his desk. "We have two house guests. They will both be in the south wing, and I don't presently know the length of their stay. The young lady may use the call button on the intercom and someone will need to go to her rooms to inquire into her needs. Meanwhile, we will all be having dinner in the dining room this evening. Four place settings, unless father arrives within the hour."

"Yes, sir," the man replied.

"Thank you," Brian said in a preoccupied manner as he started to walk away. Then he abruptly stopped and turned back. "Oh, and beef up the security on the grounds, please, and double-check the house alarms. You know what to do."

What happened in the preliminary meeting between Bunny and Katherine Sommers remained between them. Brian was curious but didn't ask any questions, although he noticed that his mother had returned Bunny's drawing to her as she emerged from his mother's study with it in her hand. Holding up one finger to excuse herself, she trotted off toward her room, presumably to put it away with the others, while Brian, Rit, and the woman of the house stood chatting comfortably with each other.

Bunny returned within minutes, and Brian then offered his arm to his mother, escorting her downstairs to the dining room and her place at the table. He held her chair while indicating with a slight gesture where Rit should seat Bunny, then himself. Brian sat in his traditional place, and a cart was rolled in bearing a tureen of steaming, delicious-smelling soup and a large serving plate piled with a selection of freshly baked breads.

Keeping a hungry and appreciative eye on the food as it was served, Rit burst out, addressing Mrs. Sommers, "Your library is great!"

The table talk was set in motion and continued amicably for an hour or more until Bunny pressed the last crumbs of her cherry cobbler into the prongs of her fork, then looking at it longingly, shook her head and set it back down on her plate.

"Does this exemplify not being able to eat another bite?" Brian asked, looking mischievously at his mother to see if there was any reaction to the cliché.

She looked back at him in mock aggravation and then asked if the two guests had everything they needed. At their affirmative, she encouraged them to call the household staff for anything they might need. Rit thanked her freely, and Bunny met her eyes with a sincere smile of appreciation. As Mrs. Sommers stood, the two young men stood up, too, and after she left the room, bidding them good night, they sat again to discuss how to get Bunny back in touch with her sister. They were deeply involved in problem solving when they both noticed Bunny's head dip and jerk up again.

"She's falling asleep right here at the table," Rit spoke softly with dismay.

"I am a most inconsiderate host," said Brian, who was also chagrined. "Let's get you to your room, Bunny." He held out his hand, and she took it like a little child, standing up slowly and allowing him to lead her to her room as Rit followed. At her door, Brian asked, "Are you sure there's nothing you will need tonight?"

Bunny smiled a sleepy smile, shaking her head.

"Okay, then I'll say good night." She wiggled her fingers at Brian and Rit, stepping inside and slowly shutting the door.

"I'll see you in the morning, okay?" Rit said as she peeked out the crack of the door, and he saw her nod before the door clicked shut.

Before going into his own room, Rit looked seriously at Brian. "Maybe I could work out a solution on my laptop. This situation is no more complex than some of the programs I've written. Well, maybe a little more complicated, but I can solve this."

"I'm glad there's an optimist in the group," Brian responded, breaking his seriousness with a brief smile. "Just kidding, Rit. If anyone can find a solution, it's you." Weariness of body and soul was overtaking him. "I'll leave you to do just that. Get some sleep, though. We'll probably need to be refreshed for tomorrow's happenings, whatever they might be." He felt like he was wearily rambling, so he held out his hand and the two shook.

"Wake me when you get up, okay?" Rit requested. Brian agreed and headed toward his part of the house.

⊰ | ⊱

A solution came to Rit in a different form than he had anticipated when he happened to see a dark car and shadowy figures slipping through the night toward the house. There was an SUV in the background that seemed safe to Rit, and he ran to Bunny's room to attempt to get her to that vehicle.

Suddenly he jerked awake, hitting the lamp next to the bed with an out-flung hand. He caught his laptop before it fell to the floor and realized that he'd fallen asleep on the bed with his computer in his lap and started dreaming. He shut down the computer quickly and pushed it under the bed. Then he jumped up to look cautiously out the window. *Wrong direction. I have to get to a window facing the front,* he told himself silently, going out into the hallway. He slipped along the walls to the foyer, where he cautiously peered out of the nearest window, across the darkened grounds toward the front gate.

19

"L et's go." Violet climbed out of bed and started dressing in the dark.

"How do you do that?" her husband asked.

"Do what?"

"Dress in complete darkness," he replied, feeling for the unfamiliar light switch.

"I think it's on the bottom section." She sounded farther away. The light came on.

"You're right."

"Always," she said, tongue-in-cheek.

He went across the room to give her a big hug and kiss. "That makes me a man most fortunate." He started pulling her back toward the bed.

"We were going where?" she inquired archly.

"Ah, yes, we were going on a different sort of adventure," he said with a deep sigh. Then he asked seriously, "Do you have that address?"

She sat on the edge of the bed with her purse in her lap, and taking out her address book, she searched for a certain listing. "Yes, here it is. You're feeling that we should definitely go over there at this time of night?"

"Let me put it this way. I don't want to, but yes, I think we should. Definitely." He had finished dressing and stood with the room's keycard in his hand. "Don't forget your shoes."

"Oh, thank you, honey. I was just about to go running down the hotel hallway without them," she responded wryly as she stepped into her shoes on the way out the door.

❈ | ❈

Carl suddenly slowed the car and shut off the headlights before turning up the lengthy driveway. Only a little ways into the property, he shut off the engine and quietly coasted to a stopping place behind some lilac bushes a little off the drive. Neither he nor Violet spoke or moved, just letting their eyes adjust to the darkness as they scanned the grounds.

Looking toward the house, Violet could barely see some movement near a car parked close to it. She whispered, "We're not the only ones up this late." Her husband gave her a quick look but didn't say anything, his eyes searching the area she pointed out. Then she spotted two figures moving from one deep shadow to another. It looked like a silent movie where people were dodging bullets in a night scene, and straining her eyes to see them better, she noticed that they were headed right toward the SUV, as if they knew it was there. She locked her vision in on them like a radar detector and finally whispered urgently, "Make sure the dome light can't turn on, Carl!"

Just as Carl hit the off switch, a back door opened and Red pushed Bunny into the truck. "I'll explain tomorrow! Go! Get her out of here," and he quickly eased the door shut and ran back into the shadows toward the house.

Carl quickly got out and pushed the truck while cranking the steering wheel around, until they were rolling back down the driveway. "Glad it slants down a bit," he grunted as he jumped back in and started the engine, edged into the street, and headed in the direction of the hotel.

He watched for several blocks to see if they were being chased but saw no evidence of it. Reassured, he briefly pulled onto the shoulder of the road to call his old precinct station and report that there seemed to be intruders on the grounds of the Sommerses' mansion. Once he was back on the road, Violet could see that he was a little more relaxed. He glanced at her and smiled. "I wish I would have had you for a partner all those years. Great night vision!"

She deliberately misunderstood. "I *have* been your partner all these years."

Carl didn't speak, just reached over and took her hand briefly, giving it an affectionate squeeze.

Bunny slipped her hand through the front seats to touch Violet's arm.

Violet patted her hand reassuringly. "We'll take you to Grace now. We're staying in a safe place."

When they arrived at the hotel, they discovered that Bunny had curled up on the back seat and was asleep, clutching her folder and an odd looking blanket in her arms.

"Oh, the poor thing," Violet said quietly. "I hate to disturb her."

"Well, seeing her sister will be good medicine." Carl leaned over the sleeping girl, softly touching her shoulder. "Come on, sweetheart, we're here. Let's go see your sister."

They helped Bunny out of the car, and Carl locked up. Then the two slowly walked Bunny into the hotel, each with a protective arm around the drowsy girl.

When they reached Grace's door, Violet knocked softly. Grace didn't seem to hear them, but Greg came out into the hallway from his room, his hair standing up all over his head. His eyes opened wider when he saw Bunny. "Great, you have her!" When Grace didn't open her door, he said, "I bet Grace is exhausted. Hold on just a sec. I have an idea." He went back into his room, and seconds later his parents heard the phone ringing in Grace's room and then a sleepy murmur as if from underneath a pillow. Greg reemerged from his room. "I only told her to come to the door."

The door opened. Grace blinked at the sudden light, but when she saw who it was, her sleepy face lit up and she quickly stepped aside, motioning them in. "Oh, thank you! Where did you find her?" Then, glancing at the lighted numbers on the clock by her bed, she added, "At this time of night!"

"What *were* you guys doing driving around this late?" Greg added.

Grace pulled back the covers on the second bed in the room as Violet led Bunny over to it, and when the exhausted girl immediately lay down and closed her eyes, Violet gently slipped off her shoes and pulled the covers up over her. Seeing the folder, she eased it out of Bunny's arms and laid it on the bedside table. "Here, it'll be right here next to you," she said softly. Then, as Bunny quickly fell into a deep sleep, she tenderly tucked the covers in around her shoulders before stepping over to where the two men waited.

Violet put an arm around each of them fondly and then smiled at Grace. "We give God the credit. For now, let's all get some rest. We can fill in all the blanks in the morning." She walked her men out of the room, giving Grace a wink as they went out the door.

⚹ | ⚹

Grace sat on the edge of her bed with a look of wonder on her face. Then she fell backward with joyous surrender. *There must be a God who cares! If you're really there, will you please let me know? I am entirely open to finding out if what they say is true. I want to thank you, if you are the one responsible for helping my sister.*

She lay still for several moments before sitting up again. As she gazed serenely at her sister's face, she noticed a funny bulge under the covers. Hoping to make her sister more comfortable, she pulled the bunched cloth out from under the cover, smoothing the top blanket, and added one more from the foot of the bed. She had started to fold up the strange cloth when the writing on it got her attention. She laid it out on her bed to see what the letters were. The cloth bore a simple geometric design, and across the bottom, in four-inch-high lettering, it said, *Jesus our Savior.*

20

Rit ducked behind the glass walls of the conservatory, hoping they might protect him somewhat from enemy eyes. They didn't. After checking around the corner and not seeing anyone, with relief he turned slowly around with his back against the glass and found he was looking into the dark eyes of a madman.

He blurted out the first thing that came to mind. "Do you guys really do suicide missions for a better place in heaven?" His next thought was, *Where is the security for this place?*

The man pressed something sharp against Rit's throat. "No talking," he whispered.

Dobermans…now. Dobermans would be a good idea. I'll have to talk to Brian about that real soon…like yesterday. He allowed kaleidoscopic thoughts into his head in order to stay calm.

Rit didn't want to die, but he decided some noise was definitely needed to alert the others in the house, so when he felt the man's grip loosen up a little, he dropped down and delivered the universal punch of pain before rolling away and jumping to his feet. Shouting as loudly as he could, he ran around the house and toward the front door. As he raced inside, he noticed the dangling wires of the alarm system before bolting up the stairs, continuing to yell as he went.

Brian burst out of his suite brandishing an antique, long-nose revolver in his hand. "What's happening?" he asked, hurrying toward Rit. In response to Rit's curious look, he added, "It's old but it fires." Brian looked in the direction Rit pointed and saw the cut wires dangling from the wall next to the alarm system keypad. He kicked off his slippers and soundlessly went toward his mother's room, gesturing for Rit to watch the stairs.

Okay, he has a gun, but I have…hands of steel, Rit told himself while staring at the front door as it began to slowly open. *It's an optical illusion, like at night when the closet door looks like it's opening by itself…I hope.* But a head appeared, surreptitiously peeking around before the figure of the stranger followed the head. Rit quickly backed into the shadows of the hallway. *Okay, so it's not an optical illusion this time.* "Watch the stairs," *Brian had motioned. I watched them, and now I'm going to…find something else to do.*

He intended on following Brian, but then another idea occurred to him. He tiptoed furtively to Brian's suite and looked around for the charger cord for his cell phone. He heard quiet steps on the staircase just as he found the cord and, pulling it to him, was disappointed to find the other end empty and caught on a golf glove. *This isn't good.* He squeezed the glove, almost wanting to cry. He renewed his efforts, spotting a possibility—a black shape on the chest of drawers—when all of a sudden, the partly open door started moving. The traditional roll-under-the-bed was the only move he could safely make, thinking in the dusty closeness how he now understood why Bunny had been trembling.

The light switched on and off again quickly. Then the quiet steps moved in the other direction. Now he'll find Brian and his mother for sure! Rit made a dive for the shape on the dresser and rolled back under the other side of the bed. He was happy to feel that the object in his hands was a phone, as he had hoped, and as he pressed a button, it lit up so he could see to dial 911. The operator answered, and softly but urgently, he started to explain the circumstances. Then the phone beeped and went dead. *Two things to tell Brian: get Dobermans and charge your phone, not your glove!* Rit felt around for the cord and snapped it onto the phone, leaving the phone under the bed as he got to his feet and crept out of the room, cautiously going where Brian had headed.

Rit was close enough to see the light under the door and hear voices filtering out into the hallway when a shot was fired. He looked around for a place to hide, but the long hallway was empty of furniture or other doors nearby, and he expected people to burst out of the room any second. The voices continued, however, and no one desperately exited, so Rit eased the doorknob around and pushed the door open just a crack, in the same way he had seen "Mr. Psycho" do earlier at the front door.

Brian's voice got louder as Rit slowly inched the door open. "…on the floor, and you kick it over here and then get down too. Oh, so you're the tough guy, huh? Just how do you plan on carrying out your mission if you're dead?"

Rit could see across a small, darkened sitting room to the partially open bedroom door. *Hope nobody else is hiding in here,* he thought as he slipped into the room and over to a position behind the half-open door.

Peering through the crack between the door and the doorjamb, he could see one bad guy getting down on the floor and another kicking a huge knife over toward Brian, who was holding his gun on them while untying his mother's hands.

Continuing to watch through one eye, Rit could see that the two men were looking at each other across the floor. Mrs. Sommers was untied and getting to her feet, and Brian appeared to be taking the rope over to the first guy on the floor. Then he saw one of the men, the same one he'd run into outside, stealthily reaching for the dagger lying there while Brian was busy tying the other man's hands and feet together behind his back. Brian's mother was trying to move toward Brian, and she was getting much too close to the unbound man on the floor. *If I jump out to stop her, Brian might shoot me, or in the confusion, Psycho might grab that dagger and use it. If I time this just right…* Rit's quick mind envisioned one scenario after another, but none of them worked without risk.

Things started into motion just as Rit had feared. Brian's mother stepped within the unbound man's reach. Suddenly he made a grab for her and simultaneously a lunge for the dagger. She did a little hop away from him just as Rit charged out from behind the door, making her scream. Brian, who was tugging at his final knot, released the rope, bringing the gun up again, this time in Rit's direction, as the assailant rolled sideways to get up. Rit felt like screaming, too, but he caught the man's shoulder with his foot, rolling him onto his back, and dropped forcefully onto his chest with both knees, pinning the attacker down.

Brian lowered the gun when he identified Rit but watched for any necessity to use the weapon without jeopardizing his friend.

"Let go of the knife," Rit demanded. The man's empty eyes stared back at him as his hand brought the knife upward with ferocious strength.

Rit's thoughts whirled as he fought a losing battle with the man's strength. *If I hadn't already had one dream this evening, I'd be hoping I was having one now.* Suddenly a huge German shepherd sprang across the room and locked the invader's arm in its teeth, snarling viciously. Falling away from the now-terrified intruder, Rit grabbed the knife even as the thought passed through his mind, *Okay, a German shepherd is as good as a Doberman.*

Rit wondered where the dog had come from as he started toward Brian. Brian's mother retreated in the identical direction, and all three huddled in amazement as the handler of the dog bounded through the doorway in similar fashion as the beast.

"Glad to find you folks. Is there anyone else in the house?" the man in uniform asked brusquely.

"Bunny's safely away," Rit murmured for Brian's ears only.

"The family is all here, unharmed. Our manager sleeps up on the third floor. Other staff are in the bungalow behind the tennis court and in the apartment over the garage," Brian informed the officer. He paused and then added tersely, "There are *supposed* to be security personnel—"

"We found someone that was drugged on the floor of an office in the back of the house. He is in the paramedic unit with the security guard we found outside. That guy took a pretty bad hit on the head. We've secured both the bungalow and the garage, and men are continuing to search the grounds, but we've found only these two perpetrators so far."

"I hope everyone else is all right," Mrs. Sommers said, her voice showing she was quickly regaining her composure, though a slight tremor betrayed how shaken she had been.

"Yes, ma'am. If we hadn't gotten the second call, we might have treated this as something more routine and not called out the full team."

"Second call?" Rit piped up.

"Yes. Just a little while ago someone reported that there might be trespassers on your grounds. Then a call from a cell phone was made that the 911 team could trace to your residence here. It was cut off suddenly, which made it top priority."

"Your cell phone is now attached to the charger," Rit informed Brian pointedly. Brian closed his eyes briefly and shook his head in something between relief and consternation.

"What is next, officer?" Brian's mother inquired, wanting to wrap it up and get all the strange men, good and bad, out of her home.

Two more police officers entered the room to remove the assailants as the officer with the dog replied, "Only paperwork, ma'am. When the men finish the grounds search, we'll be leaving. You folks can come down tomorrow to give statements."

"We totally thank you, man!" Rit said, beginning to return to normal. "Nice dog, too! Can I pet it?"

"Let me introduce you out in the hallway, okay?" the police officer agreed, and they left Brian and his mother in her rooms to talk.

"I'll have some tea sent up," Brian offered.

"No, thank you, son. There's no way anything is going to help me get back to sleep after this."

"I'll make the tea myself and join you. Would you like that?"

Pausing slightly, she then smiled and nodded her head. "Yes, I would. I'll leave a message for your father while you're occupied." She looked thoughtfully at Brian for a moment. "And, son, I was very proud of you tonight."

On his way down the hallway, Brian passed Rit, who was petting the dog, telling it what a hero it was. "Rit, I'm going to the kitchen. Do you want to join me?" Turning to the officer standing by, he said, "Thank you very much! I can't really say how much we appreciate your help tonight. Please tell the others too."

The police officer acknowledged the thanks, snapped the lead back on his dog, and headed down the front staircase. Rit followed Brian down the back stairs to the kitchen.

"This wouldn't be eerie except for how the night has gone so far," Rit commented as they walked through the dark back hallway and stepped into the blackness of the kitchen.

"You've been watching too many suspense movies," Brian countered as he snapped on a light.

"Why don't you grab the tea canister? It's in the pantry just to your left," Brian said as he moved to the stove to start heating water.

Rit opened the pantry door. Then, after a quick, mischievous look at Brian, he jumped backward with a melodramatic yell as if he'd discovered someone else hiding there.

Brian whirled around and then fell over against the counter, clutching his chest.

"Brian?" Rit said with real concern and started toward him.

"Gotcha!" Brian straightened up and laughed at the alarmed look on Rit's face.

"Very funny. You're a real funny guy."

"You started it," Brian said, returning to his task. He filled the teapot, set it on the stove, and turned on the burner underneath it. Then the two raided the big refrigerator and nibbled and talked while the water heated up.

Once they were full and calm again, Rit excused himself to head for his room, saying, "I bet I fall asleep before I get my shoes off."

"Get some good rest, Rit. Oh. Do you mind if I tell my mother about your dream? She will probably ask about Bunny," Brian respectfully inquired.

"Go ahead, Brian, that's okay. And hey, Brian, you know how to handle yourself, man."

"You don't do too bad either, Rit."

They went separate directions—Brian to talk things over with his mother and Rit to talk things over with God.

God, thanks for stepping in again. We would all be in trouble for sure without you. Please don't tell me anything else tonight, though. I'll talk to you some more tomorrow. Thanks again. Good night. Rit's heart spoke as he untied his shoes. He pulled one off and the effort sent him over backward onto the bed. *Ah, it feels good to lie down. I'll just rest here a second…*

21

At about nine o'clock in the morning, the hotel phones started jingling. Everyone checked with everyone else until all agreed to meet for brunch at eleven. The girls sat together, communing as if they hadn't seen each other for years instead of just part of a day. Greg went for a dip in the pool, hoping Grace would be similarly inclined. Violet and Carl placed some important calls and readied plans to present to the others when they met. Carl's last call was to reserve a private dining room so they could confer freely while they ate.

⊰│⊱

Violet and Carl were sipping hot coffee, and Greg was working on a cup of hot chocolate when Grace and Bunny entered the small dining room right at eleven.

"We're glad to see you, Miss Bunny!" Greg's greeting brought smiles to the sisters' solemn faces. "I want to hear everything. I bet last night was too intense."

Once orders were taken and they were alone again, they began to talk. One by one they placed their pieces of the happenings on the table, even Bunny, who was able to communicate through Grace's interpretation of her gestures. Stopping only as their food was served, they continued until all had a fairly clear picture of the last twenty-four hours, at least as far as those present were concerned.

When they had finished eating and the dishes had been taken away, Carl Johnson stood and started pacing as he addressed them.

"My wife and I made calls this morning to gather information with which we hope to make some important decisions. First let me say that I think we should all stick together." He paused to check their responses. Seeing them all nodding affirmatively, he continued. "Katherine Sommers informed us that there is no relief from the press so far. They evidently consider Bunny's phenomenal foreknowledge of the kidnapping to be so newsworthy that they are going to unusual lengths. Furthermore, there are more dangerous people who have gotten involved. Apparently some sleeper cell in this country has also gotten wind of Bunny's uncommon ability to expose their plans, and they are trying to find her. This may be what put the FBI or CIA in motion.

"The terrorists attacked Brian's home last night." When both girls started with alarm, Carl quickly reassured them before continuing. "That's all right; everyone's okay. Mrs. Sommers said she thought at first that they just wanted her, that this was still part of their original plan to lure her overseas, getting her to come to her best friend's aid so they could kidnap her and use it to put pressure on the senator." He paused, and looking at his listeners, he asked, "Are you still with me?"

When they all nodded, he went on. " Mrs. Sommers said the man's English was difficult to make out, but he demanded at knife point that she tell him the whereabouts of the girl who sees visions. She told us she feigned inability to understand, which enraged the man, but she sensed that his mission was to capture both her and Bunny alive." Carl continued the saga until all had envisioned Brian's, Red's, and the Denver police department's brave rescue.

"Now we're getting to the touchy part," he informed them. "Does anyone need anything? Coffee, water, more juice?" No one moved. "Okay, then. Who has plans for Thanksgiving?" The girls both looked puzzled, but Grace silently shook her head. "How 'bout if we relocate to a cabin up in the mountains that used to belong to a great uncle of Violet's? He passed on last year, and nothing's been done with his old place yet. He had never put it in his will, but his executor told me that Fred said his children all enjoy living in the big city now, and he'd really like Violet to have the place. He remembered her visiting years ago and how much she had loved his piece of the woods. So I've been discussing possible arrangements with the executor and last month drove up to check it out, but nothing is in writing so far—no documents that have our name or her maiden name on them. It should be hard to trace us up there as long as we're careful not to leave a trail.

"Now, don't think Aspen. Uncle Fred liked to fancy himself the last of the real mountain men and didn't believe in improvements. I'm sure it will need some work, and I'm not sure there's even electricity or plumbing up there, but that's how they used to live, and we should be able to manage. In fact, it might be kind of fun. You know, like camping out."

Everyone was perfectly still. "The only drawback is that winter's coming…soon. It's even likely that there's some snow on the ground up there already."

"Does this mean I get to chop wood?" Greg said facetiously.

"We have a volunteer!" Greg's mother joined in, grinning at her son.

"We'll stop on the way and get you some thick gloves, son," his dad promised. "What do you girls think?"

"I don't think we want to chop wood," Grace replied. "I would probably chop off something I need. We could churn butter, though, or stitch quilts."

"Okay, you guys." The big man laughed. "This won't be entirely like the pioneer days." Turning to his wife, he asked innocently, "What did I say to give them that impression?"

Violet laughed. "Honey, you're doing just fine." Then she got serious again. "May I have the floor for a moment, though?"

At his nod she pulled her chair closer to the table, absently running her finger around the rim of her cup as she spoke. "I've contacted the dean of students at the university regarding Greg's and Grace's studies—we've known each other for years. He said he'd arrange for me to get the few lessons left before finals and your final exams for you on my e-mail. That will cover your progress through the winter break. You can also register for next term via e-mail, so you basically won't lose any momentum at all."

"That takes care of us fine, Mom, but what about your job?" Greg asked.

"That's taken care of too. I also talked to the superintendent this morning, and he agreed that I could take the leave time I've accumulated. It pays to stay healthy! One of the other people in our office will take over my responsibilities until I return."

"You guys have really thought this out," Greg replied, truly sounding impressed. "Well, your plan is okay by me. What do you think, Grace?"

"I would pack up and move to the Tibetan mountains if it would keep my sister safe," Grace responded, reaching over to take her sister's hand. Bunny smiled at her and then nodded her head toward the others.

With everyone sounding agreeable, Carl resumed. "There is one more thing. It may get a little crowded." The young people all looked at him questioningly. "We mean to offer this hideaway to all the families involved."

"Uh, how big is this place, Dad?" Greg had a dubious look on his face, and his mother quickly explained that the cabin wasn't all that large, but her great uncle had raised a family of nine in it. Greg counted mentally. "We're talking about at least thirteen people—four different families!"

The longest pause of the conference ensued as everyone tried to weigh out the circumstances. "You haven't spoken to Brian or Red?" Greg asked.

"Not yet. I implied that we might have an idea when I spoke with Brian's mother on the phone, and we'll be meeting them later on," Violet replied. "I doubt that everyone will feel they need to retreat, but I think we should go over and pick up the boys, get Red's parents, and have a meeting of the minds without delay. We just wanted to bounce the idea off of you first."

Grace was the first to respond. "It's okay with us, but why is it necessary for all of us to get away?"

Greg spoke up. "I can answer that one. Now that a dangerous group of people is involved, they may try to get to anyone recently seen associating with Bunny. If they've picked up the trail the press left for them to follow, the four families are no longer safe." Suddenly turning back to his parents, he added, "Hey! What about Grace and Bunny's relatives?"

Violet replied, "I talked with your aunt this morning, Grace. She said there haven't been any strangers other than the evening you left and a few reporters the next morning. It would be good if you didn't have to return to the house for anything, though. If you could figure out a list of what you need, I'll work some way out for your aunt to get those items to you."

Grace said, "Sure. So you think they'll be okay?"

"We do, as long as they don't know anything."

Greg's dad took back over. "Well, we'd better hit the road, Violet, my newest and best partner against crime."

Rising, she addressed the young people. "See you kids later. We'll take care of everything." Taking Carl's arm, she left the room with him, her voice fading into the distance as they strolled away. "I told you. I've been your partner for all these years."

"I really love how your parents get along," Grace commented to Greg, and Bunny nodded enthusiastically.

Shaking his head but smiling, Greg looked back at the girls. "They have their moments, like every other couple, but yeah, I kind of like them too. Who would like to work out?" The girls looked a little dismayed, so he tried again. "HBO?"

"As long as it isn't a suspense movie involving terrorists," Grace said, only half-joking. "Your parents are going to be all right doing this cloak and dagger routine, right?"

"Yep. They've got supreme protection; don't worry. They'll check in to let us know they're okay," Greg answered with assurance, and offering an arm to each girl, he escorted them upstairs to their room, where they commenced channel surfing until they found something to watch that would be acceptable to all three.

⤙ | ⤚

In a few hours, just as Greg said, Violet and Carl called them from a payphone. "Hi, this is Violet. Grace? What do you and Bunny want from your house? Your aunt will meet us with your things." After a brief exchange with Grace and then Greg, they hung up, promising to be back soon.

Grace turned to Greg and inquired, "Your mom told me that they took everyone from Brian's house over to Rit's and that our relatives are staying where they are. What's the rest of it?" Bunny got up to shut the movie off and then came back to sit on the bed, watching the others' faces intently.

Greg explained. "They had a big meeting at Rit's house, and the upshot is that Rit's parents are going to visit some relatives on the east coast while Rit continues his education basically the same way you and

I will. Brian will take Mom up on her offer to help him through his finals, but his mother will join her husband in D.C."

"So, it's the five of us with your parents," Grace said after a quick mental count.

"That's doable," Greg commented.

Bunny clapped her hands together, and Grace asked, "You get a good feeling about this, Bunny?" The younger girl nodded, paused as if listening, and then nodded again.

Greg asked suddenly, "Bunny, have you been reading the Bible with my mother?" She nodded, and he went on. "Has Mom been teaching you how to listen to God?" She affirmed this also was so.

"Bunny, I didn't know that!" Grace exclaimed. Bunny wiggled her eyebrows up and down with a little grin, and Grace followed up. "I feel sort of left behind by you all." Bunny jumped up, giving her sister an enveloping hug while Greg asked for details.

"Well, I guess it sort of feels like you guys are so spiritual, and I'm…well, I don't have any special gifts from God or anything, and gee, I don't even know how to pray. Although…"

"Although?" Greg prompted.

Grace confided in them about her prayer—she wasn't sure what to call it—of the night before and how it seemed the discovery of the cloth was so coincidental.

"What a nut," Greg laughed, hugging her too. "That wasn't a coincidence. That's how God operates. Oh, and by the way, that was also a real prayer."

Bunny had gotten up to display the writing on the cloth for Greg to see.

Grace snuggled in under his arm. "Then there's hope for me?"

"More than hope. Try joy, peace—all the good stuff. Bunny, did you run to our church to hide when you left our place?" Greg had put the final piece of the puzzle together. As she nodded yes, he said, "You somehow got Red to meet you there?"

She went to the phone, picked up the receiver, tapped three times, and hung it up.

Seeing that Grace was gazing at him in awe, he said, "If only I didn't have to explain how I put all this together." He sighed and then admitted, "I figured it out because this is the altar cloth from our church."

Just then someone pounded loudly on the door, and Greg got up to peek out the little peephole. He turned around quickly, indicating that they should all be quiet. They heard the knob to the adjoining room start rattling as if someone were trying to get it open.

22

"Where on earth are those kids?" Violet was getting a little worried. Her husband was getting a room for Red and Brian while they collected some things for the trip. She had decided to check on the others, but they were nowhere to be found. Returning to the hotel desk, she stopped the transaction at the hotel desk, asking to speak with her husband privately. "Greg and the girls are missing, and I looked everywhere they might be in this hotel—*everywhere*."

Before he could respond, there was a "*pssst*" from behind a huge palm frond just behind them.

Violet started but didn't turn around. "Yes?"

"The terrorists were here in the hotel. I have my stuff and the girls' stuff. We ran to a gas station nearby, and they locked themselves in the outside washroom."

Carl spoke as if he were still talking only to his wife. "I'll get our things from the room and wait for the guys. You can go with Greg in the SUV to pick up the girls, get some things from the house—don't let anyone follow you—and then scoop us up. We might as well drive under the cover of night. Although I wish we could have rested up, we have enough drivers to rotate."

"Okay, boss," Violet said cheerfully and went toward the elevator to the hotel parking lot. Greg followed her after dislodging himself from the center of three gigantic potted palms and one large marble pillar.

"Nice touch," she said when they got on the elevator. "The hidden-voice-from-the-potted-plant thing."

"You think?" he rejoined. "Maybe we should all join an international spy ring."

"That's not even funny, Gregory."

"Uh-oh. 'Gregory,' she said. I'm in trouble."

"No, you're only in trouble if I use your middle name too." Mother and son both laughed and continued on to the car, and no one listening to the sound of their voices would have guessed how unsettled their lives had become.

⇥ | ⇤

When all three Johnsons, the two sisters, Brian, and Rit set off on their journey, the atmosphere in the vehicle was optimistic and adventuresome. Carl was at the wheel, Brian in the front passenger seat, and everyone else comfortably arranged in the two remaining seats, belongings piled high in the space at the very back.

"Let's make a burger run first, okay, gang?" Carl suggested. He looked often in the mirrors as he drove. After about a half hour, he pulled into a drive-through for fast food, and the smell of greasy hamburger filled the car as everybody munched contentedly. When people started dozing off, he had Brian open the map, and he explained the route into the mountains that they needed to take.

"Wow, that's a ways up there!" Brian exclaimed. "Would you like me to take over the wheel for a while?"

"Yep, if you would," Greg's dad responded. The moonlight lit his face with a bluish cast. "If you find your eyelids getting heavy at all, just pull over, and someone else can take it. We have plenty of licensed drivers in the group."

"Yes, sir," Brian replied respectfully. After they had stopped just long enough to switch drivers, and Carl had dozed off, Brian reflected on the whole ordeal. He realized then that he was looking forward to this adventure despite the danger and challenges. Brian searched his soul and found happiness there… and purpose.

Once during the long stretch of major highway, he thought they were being followed, but about fifty miles later, after he had exited onto a secondary highway, they had the road pretty much to themselves.

Brian pulled over a little after midnight, turning the driving over to Violet, who was fairly sure that she remembered the way to the property. Once she began driving, she realized that she was forcing her eyes to stay open, so she found a small clearing she could park the truck in, a little off the road. After unbuckling her seatbelt, which seemed so tight, she leaned her head against the door and closed her eyes.

It was the snuffling sound that woke her. In the dim pre-dawn light, she strained to locate the source of the sound. Suddenly a huge shadow appeared on her side of the car, and she found herself nose to nose with a bear, only the car window between them. Her sharp intake of breath woke her husband, who had been sleeping serenely in the seat next to her. "I wouldn't move quickly if I were you," she warned him in hushed tones, still facing the window.

"Uh, oh. Let's see…" Still groggy, he tried to focus on the problem. "It smells food. There are some leftover fries back here." He reached back and pulled the box out from behind the driver's seat. He opened his window enough to toss the fries over the top of the car and past the bear. The animal heard the box land in the leaves, and its nose twitched as it followed the scent of the food, lumbering away from the car.

"*Woweee*! That's a big one!" A sleepy voice said from the back seat.

"Huh?" A girlish combination question-yawn was heard, but she quickly added, "Bunny, wake up, you have to see this!"

Bunny, however, never saw the bear because Violet, snapping her seatbelt quickly together, pulled away right then with clods of grass flying out behind the tires. And by the time Bunny pried her eyes open, they were traveling down the road at a good speed.

Carl elucidated. "That beast finished those fries in one gulp, and he knew where they came from—you know what I mean?" All three sleepy heads nodded at the same time, and he chuckled as he turned to his wife. "What's for breakfast, honey?"

"Oh, you think I pulled over to cook breakfast, do you?"

"Isn't that what good women do in the morning?"

She swatted at him. "Now, you're the big hunter, so did you get out there and capture any game for the good woman to cook this morning?"

"I don't have to when the big game just comes to me, dear." He shrugged at their audience in the back two seats. "You see? Men rule, guys."

Greg took the pillow off his head. "What did I miss back there?"

"A huge, furry beast," Rit supplied.

"A *hungry*, huge, furry beast," Grace amended.

"Bear?" Greg shot his dad a quick look. His dad nodded. "Grizzly?" he persisted. His father nodded again.

"I could probably have eaten the whole thing for breakfast," Greg commented, trying to lighten up.

"Gross!" protested Grace, and then she stuck out her tongue.

"I bet everyone could use some breakfast soon," Violet acknowledged. "The only thing is there's no fast food up here."

Violet and her husband began to discuss their precise location and how far they were from the little town closest to the cabin, and before they had even figured it out, they saw the sign with the town's population on it.

"Three hundred seventy-four people?" Rit gasped.

Brian finally spoke up. "One town meeting and you'd know everybody's name."

"Well, here's the grocery store. Who'd like to go in?" Violet pulled into a parking place and shut off the engine. She got out, stretched, and headed inside with Grace and Bunny right behind her. The men got out, swinging their arms and shaking the kinks out of their muscles.

"Good thing you rented big transportation," Rit said to Greg and Carl.

"Yep, but we could have used a bus," Greg returned cheerfully. "You guys with me for coffee or cocoa?" The men headed toward what looked like a small café on the corner. *Open for Breakfast Only,* the sign read when they got to the door. An older woman with her gray hair in a ponytail set a coffee pot on their table without a word.

"Hot chocolate for me, please," Rit said politely.

"Could we order seven breakfasts to go?" Carl inquired.

The waitress responded curtly, "We got eggs; we got bacon, ham, grits; we ain't got no orange juice today, but hot cakes'r on the grill now, and hash browns."

"How about everything you said, enough for seven people?" Carl gave her a friendly smile. "And coffee for me and these two young men."

"All righty." Her voice sounded a little less frosty. She brought cups to fill up from the coffee pot and one hot chocolate and told them their food would take about thirty minutes.

While they waited, the men finished their drinks, and each had time to visit the tiny restroom back by the kitchen door. And true to her word, thirty minutes later, the waitress carried out brown paper bags containing boxes covered with aluminum foil. The boxes exuded a wonderful aroma, and all were much hungrier when they got back into the car.

"That hardly cost anything," Greg said to his dad.

"We may come back for an inside breakfast once we get a feel for the place—find out if we're welcome or not. Some small communities are kind of xenophobic," Carl answered.

"What is xenophobic?" Grace asked as she, Bunny, and Violet walked up with a cart full of groceries and supplies.

"Did you girls find all you needed?" Carl asked Violet as the younger men found places for the additional bags to fit in the car.

"We're fine now." Violet smiled. "Let's go see our new temporary home!"

As he got back in the car, Carl turned to Grace. "The word means 'afraid of strangers.'"

23

The twisting, rocky dirt roads weren't even marked by the time they reached the cabin, not far from town but also not very accessible. When the big SUV rolled to a bumpy stop in the yard, everyone piled out and for a moment stood just looking around them.

The cabin, clearly unused for a while but sturdy looking, stood in the middle of a clearing on a weed-covered, rocky rise above the road. Across the road, a large stand of towering lodge pole pines spread down the slope, hinting at a forest fire in the area years before. The road was lined with aspens, though by now most of their color was gone. Walking around the cabin, they saw a small barn off to one side, and near the back of the cabin, a surprisingly large pile of dry cut logs.

"You boys should be glad to see that," Carl said. "It will save us a pile of work, at least at first. Of course, it all has to be split!" He gave the young men a mischievous grin.

All eyes lit without comment on the small outhouse a little distance beyond the house, down a gently sloping path. But no one dwelled on it, as they were drawn to the view beyond. Behind the clearing was a dense, mixed forest of pine, spruce, and fir still sheltering mounds of early snow, though the open space around the cabin had melted clear in the autumn sunshine. And towering over the trees they could see the sharp rise of a mountainside nearby and a great arc of white-capped peaks, the snow cover now down to the tree line.

"Let's get the food and supplies into the house first," Violet suggested, and they all started emptying the car. Carrying in the new bags of groceries and the breakfast they'd brought from town, the women began setting up housekeeping inside. While the men did the rest of the unloading, carrying boxes and bags of additional supplies, clothing, and bedding, Grace and Bunny washed off the table and stove top, using water from a jug in the car, and set out dishes, silverware, cups, and napkins for their breakfast. Violet began putting pans and groceries in the old cupboard standing against one wall. As soon as the car was unloaded, everyone sat down and enjoyed breakfast, which was still warm.

❧ | ❧

Leaning back in the chair and feeling much better, Carl looked around the cabin and out the back window, saying, "We have a lot to do." That was a bit of an understatement, according to the expressions on the other faces, but no one looked dismayed. "Girls indoors, guys out?" He glanced at his wife.

"Okay by me. Gals?" She collected affirmative nods with her gaze, and rising from the table, Violet got the ball rolling. "We'll need water, honey," she told Carl as the men started out the door. "And if you're going to do something about wood, be sure to bring in a supply of tinder and kindling too."

"Will do," Carl said with a wave. "We'll also check in the little barn out there to see what usable tools might have been left behind. And you might want to give me time to check the chimney stacks for bird's nests before you light fires in here."

The women swept and dusted. When they began wiping the loose dirt off the windows, they discovered the caulking was so old the panes were likely to fall out, so they had to proceed cautiously. They were happy when Rit stomped in after a short while with a large pail full of water.

"Pump works; it just needed some priming." At Violet's direction, he began pouring some water into the teakettle on the stove and the rest into the wash pan in the sink. "You'll need some more, lots more," he noted, eyeing the hot-water reservoir on the stove and a big tub by the door, which had an old curtain tucked behind it that could be pulled around the whole tub like a dressing room curtain. After scanning the room for other water receptacles, he trekked off again in the direction of the pump. Meanwhile they could hear the sound of an ax thumping close by as one of the men began to split wood.

It was chilly in the cabin but not enough to hinder progress. As the sun moved around the mountain, however, the chill deepened, and Grace noticed Bunny rubbing her hands together as they placed sleeping bags and pillows on the freshly pounded-out mattresses they'd just put back on the simple, handcrafted bedsteads in the loft.

"Fingers stiff?" Grace asked.

Bunny nodded as they began climbing down the steep ladder from the loft. They were happy to see Greg and Brian coming inside with arms full of firewood, which the young men stacked neatly against the wall beside the huge stone fireplace. Greg jogged back out and in again, this time with a load of smaller pieces, which he stacked in the kitchen near the old wood-burning range. When Violet looked at him questioningly, he immediately trotted back outside and carried in an old cardboard box filled with still smaller pieces and an assortment of dry twigs and wood chips.

"Dad says the chimneys are clear," Greg reported.

Violet immediately pulled open the firebox door on the stove and began carefully laying a small pile of tinder inside and then some kindling wood. First reaching to open the damper in the chimney pipe behind the stove, she pulled a wooden match from the box she'd left on the worktable beside the stove. Bending down, she struck it and carefully held it to the tinder in the firebox, watching anxiously to see if it started burning. When it looked as though the kindling was going to ignite as well, she stood with a sigh, brushing off her hands.

"As soon as that's going good, I'll add a little more wood out of that stack you guys produced."

"Looks good, Mom."

"Yes, it's all coming back to me now." At his quizzical look, she continued, "You know, from when I was young and living in a cave, making fire and eating brontosaurus meat." When Greg chuckled, she smiled. "Seriously, I was hoping it would work. When your father first told me about this stove, I was a little worried, but I remember helping Grandma in the kitchen when I was just a child, and she had explained how she did it."

"It's a good thing. We could get awfully hungry without it." Greg grinned at her and then headed back outside, untying her apron string as he walked past.

As he followed Greg to the door, Brian added, "What I can't believe is that you actually thought to bring along an apron."

Violet laughed as she re-tied it.

Then Carl reappeared from a productive jaunt in the woods. He was carrying his .22 rifle in one hand, and with the other, he was carrying two pheasants by the feet. "I shoot, you pluck?"

"Okay, honey, but I need to ask you what became of the rest of your vocabulary. Did you leave it at home, or is it not good form for mountain men to verbalize more than two words at a time?"

"I'll look around and see if I can find some adjectives just for you. Okay, sweetie?" he replied. "Where do you want them?" He held up the birds.

She took his hand, leading him back outside, and the girls could hear her saying, "See, you *are* a great hunter. I'll cook a yummy pheasant right now."

"You'll have to cook both right now, because we don't have a refrigerator." Then their voices trailed off.

❧ | ☙

Rit finished filling the tub by the door and then turned to the women. "Where's everyone bunking?" he asked. Bunny waved for him to follow her and led him up the loft ladder. Grace heard him say, "Cool!" just as Greg burst in. He picked her up and twirled her around.

"The fresh air did you good," she said when he set her down.

"How about you? Are you happy?"

"I truly haven't had time to think about it," she stated with a little chuckle, and he insisted that she rest on the sofa while he carefully built a fire in the big stone fireplace. Soon the first tentative flames became a roaring blaze, and the two sat in the glow with warmth spreading out slowly into the reaches of the cabin.

Violet soon came in with two cleaned, plucked pheasants in her hand. First locating her roaster, placing the birds in it, and sprinkling them with some seasoning, she then grabbed a heavy hot pad and used it to open the oven door. Feeling the hot air inside and finding it satisfactory, she slid in the roaster and closed the door. Then she opened the firebox and added a little more wood before closing it up and putting down the hot pad.

Turning to the young people enjoying the fire, she said, "You girls did such a good job cleaning up this place and putting everything away. You fixed up the loft for the guys, too, right? You must be hungry."

"I'm fine. Can I help you with supper?" Grace replied, getting up.

"No thanks, honey, supper's under control. We'll just have to wait a while for our main dish to roast. But if you want to get your things situated, I put you girls in the left-hand room. The other will be for the great hunter and me." She gestured with her thumb at Carl, who had been sneaking up quietly behind her.

"Eyes in the back of her head." He shook his head with feigned dismay, "Greg—"

"Yes, sir." Greg stood up. "I bet you want help with some more firewood."

"Smart lad. How did I get blessed with such a fellow?"

"He takes after his mother," Violet retorted, wrinkling her nose at her husband. "Well…okay, maybe you had something to do with it." She gave Greg's dad a big hug. As the men went outside again, she felt behind her back. "He's better at that than Greg," she commented, reaching back to retie her apron again.

Grace giggled as she trotted off to her quarters.

⊰ | ⊱

Wonderful smells wafted through the cabin after a while, and as everyone finished whatever they had been doing, they naturally gathered in the main room. It was living, cooking, and dining areas combined, and covering much of the floor was the biggest, toughest, oblong braided rug anyone in the group had ever seen.

"Whose guitar?" Brian asked, pointing to the old acoustic guitar that had materialized in the corner. "Is it just decorative or does someone know how to play it?"

"I play a little," Carl admitted. The peanut gallery immediately demanded entertainment, so he shyly picked it up, strumming a few chords while he tried to think of something to play. After a few measures, he settled on an old hymn he thought most of them might recognize, and voices chimed in until there was a whole quartet on the last verse. The ones who weren't singing participated with enthusiastic approval.

About the time the others were running out of steam, Violet and Grace had dinner on the sturdy, hand-hewn table.

"Wow! Look at this spread!" Carl looked appreciatively at his wife. "You really didn't forget a single thing, did you?"

Violet beamed at him and then joined the others at the table. "Carl, maybe you would like to say grace tonight." As everyone bowed their heads, he thanked the Lord sincerely for the meal before them and for their safe harbor in the cabin, and then he asked for divine protection and guidance in the days ahead.

"Amen!" rang out all the voices, and then Brian looked along the table again and voiced his admiration as Carl started carving the pheasant Violet had placed before him. "Unbelievable! I'm going to love it here." A chorus of mutual assent accompanied his comment.

After dinner everyone pitched in for clean-up, putting plates in the sudsy dishpan Violet had heated with steaming water from the kettle on the stove.

Rit noticed the light was quickly fading even though it was only early evening. "Gets dark a little sooner here," he remarked, glancing at his watch.

"Indeed it does," answered Carl. "Could you fellas help me pass out the lanterns?" He dug into a big box that the men had carried in earlier and put in a corner. Inside there were battery-powered lamps that gave off excellent light. "These have a big ol' battery, but you might want to do your major studying during the day.

Maybe we can find a kerosene lamp on one of our trips to town, along with some fuel for it; that would help with evenings. We also have candles here. My only concern about them is someone knocking one over or falling asleep without extinguishing the flame, so do be careful with them.

"There is something else we will need to address too. It's soon going to get a lot colder, and we'll need to begin feeding the fireplace and stove at night. We can bank the fire at night for now, and we should be all right, but as winter sets in, someone will have to play fire keeper at night. Do we have any night owls in the group?" He looked directly at Violet, who discreetly made a face at him.

"Could I recommend that the men take turns sleeping on this couch when that time comes?" Brian offered.

"Good idea. All in favor say, 'Aye,'" Carl responded, and six cheerful ayes were said. "Okay, motion passed. Now this old man is tired, so I'll follow the old settlers' practice of following the sun to bed." He picked up the last lamp in the box and took it to his and Violet's room.

Violet set one battery lamp on the big table and went over to make sure both front and back doors were securely latched; then she lit a candle and carried it with her as she followed her husband to their room.

Bunny and Grace carried a lantern to the room they would share. Brian had the lamp for the loft, Red took a flashlight up with him, and Greg placed a flashlight on a small shelf by the back door, which led to the outhouse.

From her and Carl's room, Violet heard the tired yet satisfied tone in everyone's voices as they all called good night to one another and settled in for private conversations.

"What do you think?" She set the candle in its holder on the simple wooden stand by the bed.

"I think we have a lot of things to work out, but it's running pretty smoothly for the very first day. What do you think?"

"I think this may be the best thing that ever happened to these kids," Violet said thoughtfully.

He was silent, and she looked keenly at him after a moment. "What? What is it?"

He sighed and pursed his lips before volunteering hesitantly, "I saw some prints in the dried mud out there today."

She paused, about to blow the candle out, and turned to stare at him instead. He pursed his lips again. The meaning, Violet knew, was reluctance to speak.

"Bear?" she prompted him, also knowing he wouldn't have begun if he hadn't felt it necessary.

"Big cat...*big* cat." He clamped his lips shut, exhaling through his nose, and Violet blew out the flame without another word.

24

Lack of refrigeration was one of the hardest adjustments, but it also turned out to be a good thing. The town wasn't happy to have strangers around, but the seven newcomers didn't remain strangers very long due to the necessity of getting fresh foods fairly often. Violet used canned goods as much as possible, but everyone had a hard time doing without fresh milk, produce, beef, chicken, and bottled juice, all of which had to be used soon after purchase.

The local folks got friendlier as they became more acquainted with the newcomers. They were told that the young people were doing a project for school on communal living. This explanation for their presence was true due to the students' unanimous decision to write about the experience and submit it for credit.

The real reason they were hiding out remained private. And to protect the secret of their location as long as possible, Violet had withdrawn a large sum of money from her bank, in cash, before they left Denver so they could live a cash-only existence, and they had further resolved to use their cell phones from near the cabin only for an emergency. So far they hadn't had any unpleasant surprises.

Thanksgiving dinner was a memorable feast, like no other Thanksgiving Day any of them had ever had. The well-prepared game birds and candlelight and the sincere appreciation for life and God's gifts each one expressed was forever etched into each person's cherished memories. Christmas was a gala for remembrance as well, everyone singing carols to guitar accompaniment and exchanging little handmade gifts. After the holidays, they reevaluated their stay, and everyone had the same mind to continue a while longer in the safety of the mountains, so they settled in for the winter.

⊱ | ⊰

Once the deeper cold of winter set in, natural cold storage was possible, but when supplies did need replenishment, Carl or Brian would make the trip into town when weather permitted and the road was passable. This also gave them a chance to top off the gas tank and to make sure their cell phones stayed charged, using the charger in the SUV. During his trips into town, Carl heard tales about the large cougar that roamed the county, but he hadn't volunteered any information about the prints he'd seen except for telling the young people not to go anywhere alone or without a gun.

Violet made a trip to the Colorado Springs public library to download more schoolwork for them. She sent completed work from the post office there and picked up more pencils, paper, and folders at an office supply store, and lastly stopped at a hardware store for some items to help with the biology labs. Just before leaving the store, she remembered to purchase the light bulb for her microscope, which needed replacing.

Violet smiled to herself on the way home as she recalled how the rather cool and suspicious waitress at the breakfast café in town had grudgingly acceded to their use of an outlet near one of the tables for breakfast labs. Then the woman's curiosity brought her closer and closer to their projects until she quite enjoyed sitting with them if there weren't any other customers.

All in all, the living situation was working to everyone's satisfaction. The students were making progress with their studies and learning independence and responsibility as well. Everyone stayed healthy too, and the young men enjoyed the way their strength and endurance increased through their new vigorous lifestyle. "Better than a gym!" was Greg's description of chopping wood. Violet's prediction that it would do everyone good seemed accurate until one day in late February, when Bunny had another prodigious vision.

⛧

It was a particularly cold morning, but the sky was clear and the road was in unusually good shape, so Greg and Grace had joined Brian for a trip into town for eggs, soap, fuel for the truck, and as a welcome treat, fresh milk. Carl was going hunting. Game was scarcer now that winter had taken over, but he thought he might scare up something for a change from the frozen meat they often relied on.

Violet had just waved to the three in the SUV and kissed her husband good-bye, urging him to be careful, when she turned back inside and observed that Bunny was staring fixedly at the stone wall of the fireplace.

For someone to daydream while staring at the fire itself wouldn't have seemed strange, but the direction of Bunny's unfocused gaze struck Violet as peculiar. Drawing closer to investigate, she perceived that Bunny was having another revelation. She motioned to Rit, who was descending the ladder from the loft, to make little noise, and as he complied, the two moved toward the kitchen table, where they could speak softly together.

"Is this what a vision-haver typically looks like?" Rit inquired.

"Everyone is probably different, Rit." She went on to explain what she understood about her heavenly Father and how He, while encouraging individuality, also lovingly guides his children toward a joyful, successful life. Rit had a lot of questions during their conversation regarding hunger, pain, and suffering. Violet fielded them to the best of her understanding, focusing on how God's love prevails, even though humankind's twisted ways and cruel intentions have made a tough course for some of God's children to get through. "If God interfered with man's intentional will, then His whole premise of loving Him and choosing Him through free will would be negated." Violet ended there.

"We would be *programmed*," Rit said, indicating his dawning comprehension.

"Exactly! Contrary to what a lot of people think, God's plan is to free us through our own self-control, choosing His power in our lives, to be the people we want to be—loving, happy, peaceful—"

Her sentence broke off as Bunny approached the table, urgently showing Violet the broken tip of her pencil. "Don't worry, we have a sharpener somewhere. Are you going to draw what you saw again, my dear?" Bunny nodded as Violet went to a basket of miscellaneous items sitting on the kitchen worktable. "We've collected quite a few things in this catchall. Oh, here's the sharpener." She handed the pencil sharpener to Bunny, who almost ran back to her place on the sofa, where folder and more paper were lying, having been collected without Rit or Violet noticing.

"Intense conversation," Rit commented with a grin. Violet smiled back as she started to prepare their midday meal. "Need any help?" Rit asked.

"Maybe we could use a little more wood in this pile here," she replied, indicating the stack by the stove.

"Yes, ma'am." Rit cheerfully went for his jacket, but as he passed Bunny, he glanced over her shoulder and completely forgot about the wood. "Violet! I think you need to see this right away!"

Something in his tone made Violet drop the paring knife and potato into the sink and rush over to the sofa. In the sketch Bunny was hastily finishing, her husband was depicted face down in the snow with what had to be the elusive cougar on his back. Rit scampered up the ladder, shouting over his shoulder, "I know where he goes to hunt sometimes!"

Violet grabbed her coat and a shotgun, taking several shells out of the box on a nearby table and stuffing them in her pocket. "Please lock the door after us, Bunny," she called on her way out.

Rit jumped from halfway down the ladder to the floor and sped out the door into the snow. Stopping only to load the shotgun, they hurried toward the trees. With Rit estimating the general direction he'd gone, the big man's boot prints were easy to find once they left the yard.

The two of them pushed through the snow with urgency, clouds of vapor rising above their heads at every breath. They heard a rifle shot close to them as they forged through the deeper snow up an incline, and when they were able to see over the top; the whole awful scene was laid out in front of them. Violet gasped and tried to run down the slope, falling in the snow several times and pressing on again without thinking about herself. Rit followed and caught up as she got to her husband, who was lying face down in the snow. Rit snatched up the shotgun from where she'd dropped it as she fell to her knees and fired in the direction of the large cougar, which was tearing into a deer that was lying fairly close by. Violet quickly handed him six more shells before bending over Carl and carefully turning him over. She caught her breath when she saw that his head had hit a rock and the arm tucked underneath him had been mauled by the big cat.

Rit reloaded, and running closer, fired both barrels. The cat cast him an insolent look and then ran into the forest at a leisurely gait, stopping once to lick its paw and gaze back at them. Rit, inserting more ammunition into the chambers, blasted at the predator again, forcing it to retreat out of sight.

"We won't be eating that deer," mumbled Carl as he held a glove full of snow on the rising lump on his forehead.

"Shhh," Violet cautioned him, "let's help you up now. Can you walk?"

"Yep," her husband replied, but he staggered a bit as he tried to rise. Looking at his arm, he stated flatly, "He got me, but it could have been worse. Violet, you steady me. Things are still somewhat fuzzy."

"Isn't it kind of hard to tell what fuzzy is in all this snow, dear?" This time her teasing covered the fear she felt as she saw her husband struggle to rise and steady himself on his feet. "Maybe that's why I can't quite tell where the ground is from the sky," he replied with a weak grin. "Violet, could you hand me that rifle?" He gestured toward the weapon he had dropped in the snow. Taking it from her and using it like a cane, he took a couple of tentative steps before turning to the teenager now anxiously watching. "I can do this, Rit, but will you watch our backs with that shotgun?"

Rit immediately turned so that he was walking sideways in order to see in front of and behind them as they struggled through the deep snow back to the cabin.

⇥ | ⇤

Bunny had situated herself in a chair near a window, sketch paper in hand, in order to watch for them. As she waited, she continued her drawing but kept an eye on the edge of the forest. Once she spotted them coming, she jumped up to unlock the door and throw it open for the trio to stagger into the cabin.

When they were inside, Violet helped Carl to a seat and then carefully removed his now-tattered shirt, examined his injured arm, and decided it needed medical attention. While they waited anxiously for the return of the people who'd gone into town, Carl expounded on the miraculous appearance of the deer that drew the cougar's attention away from the hunter who had apparently been "the hunted."

"I don't know how long that cat had been stalking me, but just as I sighted the deer, I felt that big thing land on my back. I got my shot off, though, before I fell, and as the buck started to go down, the cat went for the deer." He shook his head in amazement, especially when he saw the sketch that brought them so quickly to his aid. Then he closed his eyes, drifting off to sleep.

Violet sprang into action. "Don't let him fall asleep just yet, not with that bump on his head. Will you talk to him, Rit ? Ask him to tell the story again, and I'll make some coffee."

They were running out of ways to stop Carl from nodding off when the others returned with supplies. They were appalled to find such an emergency awaiting them, and everyone quickly joined in helping the large man into the SUV. Then Greg and his mother got in on either side of Carl, Brian took the wheel, and they quickly took off.

"I'll watch over the girls," Rit called as the truck barreled out of the yard and back down the road. Turning back to Grace and Bunny, he said, "Good thing that cat has a nice, big buck to eat, so it won't come for you!" He growled, clawing the air in front of their faces.

"Not funny," Grace said. Bunny shook her curls and, putting her nose in the air, turned her face away.

"Oh, come on, give me a break. I'm trying to cheer you up." His charm won out as they all linked arms and went inside to sit by the fire.

"What else did you draw, Bunny?" Rit asked his silent companion.

She handed over three sheets of paper. One was the finished picture of the event that had just occurred. The next was a picture of the president talking on the phone, with phone lines connecting to a group of people who sat with a banner over them that said *UN*. In the shadows behind the president, there was a clear portrayal of a prominent Middle Eastern leader standing behind another man, who in turn was holding a knife poised to strike the president in the back. The third sketch was simple; there were two portions of land separated by an ocean, and over the ocean was a missile heading west.

Rit and Grace were speechless. Bunny looked from one to the other hopefully until Grace said, "We have to do something!"

Bunny nodded encouragingly, but silence enveloped them again like an overpowering wave.

Rit only spoke to break the despondent hush. "But what? What can we do?"

25

Violet gave the hospital their insurance information without hesitations then whispered in her husband's ear, "We just need to think about getting you fixed up right now." He went to sleep sitting in the hospital wheelchair as they waited for the nurse to roll him into the emergency unit, but the nurse assured Violet that they would take good care of her man, and the long wait ensued.

Brian left to take home the local fellow they picked up when they passed through town. When they'd asked him where the nearest hospital was, the man had replied, "Kin show ya better than tell ya," and after jumping in, he did just that. The hospital wasn't very far from town, but a person surely had to know where it was to find it.

Dusting the snow off his coat as he reentered the emergency room waiting area, Brian said, "Thank God for four-wheel-drive! Our guide preferred not to go back to town but rather to his house, which had less road than we have. How is our fearless leader?" He asked this lightly, but concern shone in his eyes as he directed his question to Violet. The doctor walked in before she could speak.

"You are Mrs.—" the doctor asked.

Violet nodded as she quickly got to her feet.

"Your husband's injuries are pretty straightforward. He does have a concussion, and we're working on the arm right now. I expect him to recover nicely, but I want to keep him under observation overnight, if that's okay." Violet nodded yes again.

"I'll stay with you, Mom," Greg volunteered.

"There's no need for you to do that, Greg. Why don't you and Brian go home and get some rest. My place is here. We'll be fine." She was firm, so after hugs and farewells, the two young men left while Violet was shown to the room her husband would occupy.

Greg was silent as Brian drove them back to the cabin, simply gazing thoughtfully out at the moonlight sparkling on the snowy world that encompassed them.

"You okay, Greg?"

"Yes…well, no, not really." After a brief pause, Greg began pouring out his heart while they drove, speaking about the invincible image he'd always had of his father and how this incident had shaken him up. The two young men became even better friends that night.

When they pulled up in front of the cabin, they were surprised to see the kerosene lamp was still lit. As they came through the door, the other three crowded around them even before they got their coats and boots off, Grace and Rit talking at the same time, Bunny waving her sketches in the air.

"Wait, wait a minute. Okay, one at a time." Brian tried to sort things out. After the new developments were made clear, Greg and Brian understood why no one was able to sleep.

"Three times now you've been verifiably accurate," Brian said thoughtfully. "I think we could approach the president with those figures."

"If we made copies of all the sketches so far and put together a file with an explanation of the one hundred percent accuracy of the ones that are confirmable, we could send it tomorrow," contributed Rit.

"What about the postmark?" Greg asked. "And won't they think it's odd if we don't include a return address, phone number, or even e-mail address?"

"I'm getting a headache," inserted Grace, and everyone turned to her with sympathetic expressions that made her burst out laughing. "Someone should take a group picture of you guys." The small bit of humor loosened up the tension, and they all agreed that rest would be good for them. The problem would still be there for them to work on tomorrow.

When the men were all in their loft resting place, Rit's voice came out of the darkness. "I just can't help thinking…" There was a long pause.

"Okay, I'll ask," Greg responded. "*What* are you thinking?"

"Maybe I shouldn't say."

"Now you have me curious too, Rit," Brian joined in. "What is it?"

"I probably shouldn't say it." A bombardment of pillows flew in Rit's direction, and he laughingly tossed them back. "You'll probably want to throw them again if I say it."

Both voices growled his name.

"Okay. What if there *is* no 'tomorrow'?"

There was no second volley of pillows. Indeed, there was no response at all. Each of the three lay awake a long while, though, until at last they each restlessly dozed off. And right before dawn, Rit started dreaming.

He woke up with a troubled heart. The problems with the sketches, nuclear disaster, the threat of personal danger to the president or to an important policy he was working on—the ideas swirled like a tornado in Rit's mind. Then he spotted the shadow. It looked like two people struggling, one person's hand over the other one's face or mouth. And then it was gone. He ran outside, but he didn't see anything in any direction. He yelled out names—

"Rit !"

Someone called him. "Where are they? I can't see them." He started to panic as he jerked awake with Brian's face looking closely at him.

"You all right, bud?" Brian asked, "Dreaming or something?"

"Huh?"

"You called my name. It woke me up, not that I was sleeping very well anyway, thank you," Brian said with a rueful smile. "It's nice to wake up to another day, though."

"Uh, thanks, man. I was dreaming, I guess." Rit's eyes adjusted slowly to the soft light of dawn. Sitting up, he ran his hands through his thick hair. Glancing across the loft, he noticed Greg was still sleeping undisturbed, his blankets rising and falling peacefully.

"Poor guy," Brian commented. "He's got a lot to bear right now. Do you want to join me for breakfast, or do you want to try to get more sleep?"

"No," Rit answered quickly. As tired as he felt, he didn't want to fall asleep. "Breakfast sounds good, Brian. Let's go."

Over breakfast Brian invited Rit to tell him about the dream that was so obviously upsetting. "We need to pay attention to those dreams of yours just as much as Bunny's visions," Brian urged, and Rit detailed the brief but disturbing dream.

After he finished, they sat in silence, both having a feeling of being beset with troubles, like people feel after days and days of rain with no sunshine at all. Grace and Bunny joined them presently, looking more refreshed but somber. Laying her folder on the table, Bunny took a seat, and Grace made a light breakfast while the plans they discussed swirled, finally gelling by the time a sleepy-looking Greg climbed down.

He listened sagely while munching on a bagel. Then, standing up, he said firmly, "Let's do it!"

They drove straightaway to the hospital. While Greg went to his father's room, Brian asked to use the copier in the hospital office. Bunny and Grace waited respectfully with Rit, to be invited to visit after Greg had a chance to talk with his dad privately.

After a short time, Violet found them in the waiting room and waved for them to follow her. She seemed like a bright and cheerful mountain flower, the kind that grows even out of the merest crack in solid rock. Her presence lifted the young people's spirits as she chatted about her husband's condition and listened as they told her about the recent happenings at the cabin.

They found Carl sitting comfortably on the edge of his bed, all dressed and with a sling on his arm and a bandaged head. When he saw their curious looks at the bandages, he chuckled. "My head's too hard to break, but I did have to have a couple of stitches up there too. Anyway, now I'm just waiting to speak with the doctor, and then I'm outta here!"

Just then Brian walked in with the drawings and copies. Violet reached out for one stack, so giving the originals to her, Brian handed the copies to her husband. As they scrutinized the sketches, Greg expounded on "the plan."

"Sounds good," Carl said approvingly, and Violent nodded in agreement.

When the doctor came in, everyone left the room except Violet, but after milling around in the hallway for a short while, they saw the doctor, Carl, and Violet coming out of the room. Carl was walking a bit stiffly, but he was smiling and making an okay sign with his hand. Greg went out and brought the truck up to the door, and they left the hospital with smiles all around and heartfelt thanks to the staff.

After dropping the older couple off at the cabin, where they could get some real rest—Carl had told them humorously about "those nurses waking me up all night just to ask if I was okay"—the young crowd headed for Colorado Springs where they'd decided it would be safe enough to mail the package to the White House.

⊰⊱

The first stop was the public library where Grace, Bunny, Greg, Red, and Brian all used the library's computer area to compose a cover letter by consensus. The letter included a description of the events that had led up to their evacuation from Denver, a verification of the events that Bunny had predicted, and places for the signatures of all the witnesses present. Once they were satisfied, they printed it out and signed it. They mailed their package with the feeling they were small and helpless against terrorism, but they knew that if someone would listen to and act on the evidence, there might be a chance of salvation. In this mixed frame of mind, they drove back to their hideaway.

⊰⊱

The next couple of months were spent taking care of Mr. Big, as the young people had affectionately started calling Carl. Greg, Brian, and Rit worked hard to finish their courses on time. Grace and Bunny kept up scholastically and enjoyed the camaraderie with their peers and, in a unique way, their growing relationship with Violet. They had never had a close relationship with a mother before. For the same reason, they had never had anyone teach them domestic skills, and they were delighted to be learning so much from Violet as they helped with the running of this new household. In addition, the two sisters grew even closer. Brian, Rit, and Greg took up the task of hunting for meat, and the group never lacked anything they needed. There were no more wild animal attacks, no nuclear bombs fell from the sky, and no terrorists or reporters were seen lurking around.

In fact, their simple life was very peaceful until a misty day near the end of April, when stillness lay over the countryside, and in the early light near dawn, everything was a muted gray.

26

Rit woke up suddenly. He had a hard knot at the pit of his stomach and a sense of rising anxiety. It took him a few seconds to realize that he was not physically ill; rather, he was emotionally anticipating something. "What?" He hardly knew he had spoken aloud as he jumped out of bed, climbed down the ladder, and went to the window facing the yard. Peering out into the gloom, he saw the struggling shadows of his dream. Shouting for help but not waiting for it, he stuffed his feet into some shoes at the door, grabbed the shotgun and some shells, and ran toward the barn, where he'd last seen the two figures.

They weren't anywhere in sight when he arrived, and because the snow had melted from the clearing, there were no clear tracks to indicate their direction. He carefully circled the barn, going inside to poke around in the old, stale hay before coming back out to stare up into the sky with exasperation. There was the morning star, the only star left in the sky, a prelude to dawn. As he calmed himself in its beauty, he heard low voices. Rit turned just in time to spot three silhouettes rapidly disappearing among the trees directly behind the cabin. The one in the middle was Bunny.

He ran back toward the house to meet Greg, emerging by leaping from the doorway to the ground in his haste, ignoring the steps. "What's going on, Rit ?"

"They've got Bunny! Right over there! We have to catch up *now*!" Rit waved his hands in the air. "This shotgun's no good. They've got her too close. Come on! Come on, let's go!"

Brian burst out of the house with the rifle in his hand. "What's going on out here?"

Carl appeared in the now lighted doorway. "What's going on? Is it that cougar again?"

Rit yelled emphatically, "They've got Bunny! Let's go!"

Greg, who had peered very strangely at Rit's feet while all the shouting was going on, had scuttled inside and now came back out of the cabin with an armful of shoes. "Rit, not only do you have two left shoes on, but one of them is mine," he stated. "If I'm going to do some chasing, I'd rather have my own shoes—a right one *and* a left one."

Rit muttered something under his breath that no one could quite hear as he went back to the steps to sit down and straighten out the shoe dilemma. Then he stood again, leaning the shotgun carefully against the doorframe and insisted, "Okay, let's *go*!"

"Wait for me!" a high voice stopped them just as they were leaving the clearing, and Grace came running up. She was wearing a backpack and had a canteen slung over her shoulder, and she carried an armful of jackets. The young men gratefully put the jackets on, since it was a very chilly morning. As they all headed into the trees, Brian asked, "What's in the backpack?"

"Violet and Mr. Big put some food in there. She won't let him come with that arm. They sent along water too." She held up the canteen that hung at her side.

"Here, let me carry that backpack." Greg gently removed it from her shoulders as they hurried along.

Brian stepped up to take the canteen. "I'll take this. Stuff like this can get heavy if we end up walking a while."

And walk awhile they did, first trying to find the trail in the occasional patches of snow and then struggling to keep track of it as it wound through the trees. Occasionally finding a freshly broken tree branch, and once a piece of Bunny's heavy bathrobe, encouraged them, showing them they were on the right path. And all the while they went on, they were constantly climbing.

Eventually they noticed the trees around them were growing sparse and less tall. When they finally crested a ridge and stopped to catch their breath, they found that the ground dropped sharply away on the other side. Below them they could see a deep ravine and just make out what looked like parallel dirt tracks along the bottom—a road.

"Hey, look over there!" Rit whispered urgently, pointing to one side of the track below them. "I'll bet that truck belongs to Bunny's kidnappers! Do you suppose that's where they're trying to take her?"

"I'll bet you're right," Greg said, "but they're sure going to have a tough time getting down to it from up here. They must know of some other way, maybe a long way around."

The men all looked at each other silently.

Finally Greg said, "It's a risky trail, and I'm probably not the best climber, but I know engines and how to stop one from working. I'll go."

Pulling off the backpack, he started down the almost vertical drop to the hidden road below. The remaining three watched with concern as he slipped, catching trees to regain control of his descent. Just as Greg was about twenty feet from the bottom, he slipped off a large rock in his path and started rolling head over heels down the slope. He finally came to rest lying on his back right by the front tire of the truck. From their high viewpoint, his audience could see his chest heaving and waited anxiously to see if he was all right. But then he gave a faint wave to indicate that he was able to continue his mission and slid under the truck for five minutes before reemerging with some parts in his hands. He carried them into the trees and buried them here and there under small rocks and beneath the tree litter covering the ground.

After he finished, he stepped back onto the track to make sure his work was invisible. His watchers saw him stiffen and seem to listen and then hurry back into the trees out of their sight. Alerted to danger by Greg's actions, the others quickly dropped to the ground and lowered their faces into the weeds, but they kept close watch below. In a moment the two men and Bunny came into view, marching down the rutted road from the other direction.

"Not daggers this time," Brian whispered to Rit, who looked more closely and also observed the automatic weapon hanging on the back of one of the men. The other man had a hand cupped under Bunny's elbow as they walked her toward the truck. When they reached the truck, the man with the weapon grabbed her arm and pulled her around to the passenger side, opening the door and pushing her in while the other man got in behind the wheel.

When the driver tried to start the truck and found he couldn't, he got out again and lifted the hood, speaking loudly in another language as he poked around, looking for anything that might have come loose. Then he angrily slammed down the hood and looked around with narrowed eyes.

The three young people on top of the ridge flattened out and inched a bit farther back out of view. They heard him holler something to the man in the truck, and two doors opened and slammed. There were scuffling noises and the rise and fall of angry voices.

Rit put his mouth as close to Brian's ear as he could without tickling and whispered softly, "Should we try to get her now?"

"I'm not that good a shot yet. Are you?" Brian turned his head just enough to see Rit out of the corner of his eye.

"No, but if we track them, we might lose her or lose the element of surprise if they catch on."

"Not with the help of God," Brian said. He surprised himself a bit with that; he hadn't even been aware of such trust in God and the strength that came with it growing inside him.

It became quiet on the road below, and Brian crept forward again for a little peek. He saw the three trudging back down the road the way they'd come, and from his bird's eye view, he also noticed that Greg had come out from wherever he had been hiding and was crouched behind the truck, peering out at Bunny and the men as well. Brian and Greg made eye contact, and Greg signaled that he would follow immediately behind them. Brian indicated that he would try to pick up the trail on the ridge, and everyone got in motion.

Rit put on the backpack. "We have the water and food."

"Greg will be okay for a while," Brian assured his troupe. "Let's try to figure out where they are. We'll sneak up on them at the right moment and get Bunny back. Try not to get separated."

The plan seemed to work. Along the way Brian discovered that Greg knew some birdcalls. Greg used the calls to guide Brian closer, letting him know that he was still right behind Bunny.

As the trio on the ridge continued, they saw that the slope to their left was becoming less extreme, and they began slowly working their way downward as they went, moving in the direction where they believed the road was. After a short while, Rit cautiously took a look around a big rock and found that they were now nearly on the same level as Bunny and her kidnappers. Continuing to watch for a moment, he saw the man with the gun whip it down into position and turn in a circle, muttering to the other man. The other man was still pulling Bunny along. As Rit watched, he responded to his partner's comments by making a bad imitation of one of the calls Greg had used. "They're psyched out about all the whistling," Rit buzzed in Brian's ear.

Brian breathed softly, "Shh…we're too close." He was right. The wind carried the little comment directly to the ear of the enemy. The man pointed the gun straight toward them and started walking in their direction. "Well, we might as well say anything we want to now, Rit." Brian leveled the rifle defensively while Rit went around the rock the other way.

Greg crept up stealthily behind the kidnapper who held Bunny until he was only a few yards behind him. Then he suddenly dashed forward, surprising the man, who yelled as Greg jumped onto his back, which allowed Bunny a moment to pull away and run. To everyone's surprise, though, instead of running toward the rock that had concealed Rit, Grace, and Brian, Bunny ran toward the man with the automatic rifle, now pointed at Greg, waving her hands in the air. All the men stared at her, but the first to take the advantage was Brian, who charged out from behind the rock and knocked the armed man out with the butt of the rifle before he could even turn around again. Rit had rushed to Bunny's side, intending to help her away from all the action, but she knelt beside the unconscious terrorist with a distressed look on her face. She placed her hand gently on the back of his head as if trying to undo the huge lump that was forming. Then accepting Rit's assistance to her feet, she let herself be led over behind the rock. When she saw Grace, she ran into her arms, and they hugged each other with tears of joy and panic mixed together.

Meanwhile the young men confiscated the automatic rifle and took control of the situation by motioning the other kidnapper, who was wrestling fiercely with Greg, to lie on the ground. The man dropped to the earth with reluctant compliance.

"You must have run a good fifty-yard dash in track and field, Brian," Greg stated while getting to his feet.

"And you must have hit a few home runs too," Rit added, coming back to stand guard over the still unconscious kidnaper.

Brian closed his eyes briefly with a modest smile and shake of his head.

"Now what?" inquired Greg.

"I really don't know," Brian replied.

"Let's tie them up," Rit suggested.

"With what?" practical Greg asked.

"Let's just hit the other one on the head and run." Grace's contribution sounded unexpectedly tough, coming from such a sweet young woman, and when Brian said as much, she just arched her eyebrows and set her jaw.

"With what?" Greg asked again, not letting any sideshows deter him from the subject at hand.

Bunny approached, proffering the belt of her bathrobe. "Hmm. Nice and strong, fuzzy, tough enough to hold them but not too hard on their wrists," Rit commented.

Greg rolled his eyes upward with a sigh.

Brian approved the idea but not the item. "Actually, Bunny, you may still need that, but what might they have in their pockets?" Brian and Greg proceeded to search both men's pockets and eventually found some zip ties in one inside jacket pocket. "What do you think?" Brian held them up, looking at his friends over the unconscious man's lolling head.

"Maybe they thought they'd need them to control Bunny." Greg's tone indicated how ludicrous he thought that concept was should it be true.

"Maybe they're just standard issue?" was Rit's droll contribution after which Brian, tight-lipped, gestured for the conscious man to crawl on his stomach to a tree, and with Greg propping the other one up, Brian tied them tightly together using their own zip ties.

Then he sighed and stood brushing off the tree needles that clung to his pants legs. "I wish we could speak that guy's language," he said after a pause. "We could maybe tell him about Jesus so he could have a more peaceful existence. These men don't even truly follow the teaching of the Koran. I gained some insight from a missionary recently who said there are references in the Koran to another book with more wisdom. We felt it may be pointing to our Scriptures."

⊰│⊱

They had intended to get back to the cabin and call the authorities, to let them know about what had happened and where they'd tied up the bad guys, but Grace, Greg, Rit, and Brian had all been so intent on the rescue attempt that they couldn't find their way back. This fact dawned on them slowly. At first the trail back seemed familiar and they were able to follow the same kinds of signs they'd used while searching for Bunny, but somewhere along the way they got lost and then more lost.

"You know, a person hears about other people getting lost in the mountains, but—" Rit began.

"Don't even start. We're not lost," Greg said firmly.

"You're in denial, man," Rit remarked. "A person never thinks it will happen to them. I think we need to come up with a plan, especially since we're pretty high up here." Looking ahead of them, they could see barren mountainside, steeper than anything they'd covered yet, the only passage along it a narrow and treacherous-looking natural shelf in the rock.

They looked doubtfully at the way ahead.

"If we can get past that rock outcropping, it should be better on the other side. And we should find a way back downhill at some point," Greg offered optimistically.

"How many vote for going forward?" Brian looked around as everyone put a hand in the air.

Then it started to snow.

27

Bunny's thoughts swirled like the snowflakes around her. The sudden spring storm had separated Grace and her from the others, and she felt like it was her fault. As she leaned her weary head back on the rocky mountain, she was all too aware of the void before her, the mountainside dropping away just a little beyond her toes.

She concluded that she had a recurring problem in her life. Every time there was trouble, she withdrew, allowing only Grace partial access. She recalled the day Mama was beaten. She felt the beating was her fault, so much so that she never said another word that would get anyone else in trouble. She remembered being huddled under the church pew and a very concerned Rit trying to draw her out. And now, when the snowstorm had blinded them as they made their way along the narrow trail and their group tried to form a more secure line by joining hands, she'd pulled away at a crucial moment, placing Grace and herself in danger.

Bunny pulled her heavy robe more tightly around herself, shivering. Her bare ankles ached. She could hear Rit's voice calling out an explanation to Brian at the front of the line. *It should only take them a minute or so to retrace their steps and find us.*

She thought back to this morning. Waking before dawn this morning, she'd pulled on her robe and shoes and quietly let herself out the back door and made her way to the outhouse. She had just started back up the path to the cabin when an indistinct figure had suddenly emerged from the shadows, grabbed her, and clamped a rough hand over her mouth, making it hard for her to breath. She'd struggled as he dragged her toward the barn, frightened as never before, but when she heard Rit shouting for the others, she felt the rising of hope that they would rescue her.

Her attention returning to the present, she began to shiver uncontrollably. Rescue her they had, but then they had all become lost while trying to get back to the cabin. Now she and Grace were stuck on this narrow ledge, alone and unable to see their way. All her thoughts flashed before her in seconds.

Then things got worse. Grace tried to place her arm around Bunny to warm her, but in the attempt to get closer, Grace accidentally stepped off the now invisible path. As Bunny grabbed onto her sister, she too was pulled off her feet, and the two rolled down the side of the mountain, stopping only when they reached the bottom of a narrow, steep-sided ravine.

They landed close to each other. The stop knocked the wind out of Bunny, but when she caught her breath, she found she could move all right. Rubbing the snow out of her eyes, she got to her knees and moved closer to her sister. Grace wasn't moving. Bunny shook her slightly, then frantically brushed the snow off her to see if there were any bones that didn't seem right.

Suddenly she heard voices cutting in and out around the wind's awful howling.

"…they…right here…last saw…"

"…down further…they might…"

The voices started to fade. Bunny needed to cry out. She felt a horrendous pressure building up inside her soul, the necessity of trying to save her sister pushing against years of silence felt like a tidal wave overpowering a port city. Her stronghold of resolve crumbled in front of the wave of loyalty and love as she leaped to her feet, opening her mouth to scream, "We're here!"

The noise that came out didn't disturb even the tiny bird huddled on a branch a foot away from her, its feather fluffed against the cold. It only stared at Bunny. She tried again and again, but the vocal suppression throughout her early years had diminished her capability to call out at will, and she collapsed in tears when she could no longer hear the faintest whisper born on the wind from her friends above.

She wept, the salt from her tears dissolving the snow in front of her into an odd-shaped hole. When the tears stopped, Bunny crept to Grace's side to curl up against her, sharing warmth. She noticed the wind had dropped and the snowflakes were fewer and further apart, and the lazier way they fell from the sky made her feel sleepy.

⇥|⇤

The men went beyond where they had last seen the two young women. The elements and their fears worked on them until dread threatened their souls as the sun sank behind the mountain peaks.

Greg found a wider place, carefully testing the ground with his feet before sinking to his knees and crying out, "God! We need you like never before. You know where they are, and we don't." His cry ended in a painful moan as he bent low, dropping his forehead onto his fists in the snow.

Rit peered at Greg with distressed eyes as Brian laid the rifle down and raised his eyes toward heaven, holding his hands outward speechlessly. All three were a picture of fervent need as the helicopter came around the shoulder of the mountain.

"Wow, Greg! You got a fast answer, man." Rit held onto a bush growing out of the rocks beside him.

Brian took charge, waving his arms and shouting to make sure the rescuers had spotted them. He quickly grabbed the lifeline as it was lowered within their reach. "Rit, you and Greg go up, and I'll work my way back to where we thought we lost them on this ledge." He snapped the harness swiftly around Rit and signaled the co-pilot, who reeled him in.

Brian could see Rit explaining the plan to the crew, and the process was repeated, getting Greg safely aboard as well.

As the two of them scrutinized the area from their new vantage point, Rit suddenly shouted, "Look! A heart in the snow! And there they are!" Pointing excitedly as the helicopter dipped, everyone leaning to see what he'd discovered, Rit guided them right over the place the two girls were lying with a light snow blanket over their clothing and a dent shaped like a heart at their feet, now filling up with snow.

"That ravine is deep and we don't have that much cable. Looks like we need paramedics too. I'll radio for a better-equipped unit." At Rit's concerned expression, the pilot continued, "Don't worry; they'll be here in ten minutes."

With Greg serving as spotter from his aerial vantage point, Brian sat down and slid from his perch on the trail and down the mountainside, tumbling almost on top of the sisters before stopping himself short by sheer strength and determination. He caught a package of HEAT the chopper let down and released, placing it quickly between Bunny and Grace. Not knowing what they may have broken on the way down, he didn't move them but lightly rubbed extremities, working tirelessly, rotating from feet to hands, to the next one's feet and hands. His efforts were rewarded when Bunny began to stir, slowing opening one eye. She moved her lips. Brian quickly bent closer to her with the incredulous thought that he heard a whisper come from her lips before her eyes closed again. *It had to have been the wind…just the wind*, he decided as he continued his ministrations.

⊰ | ⊱

The first helicopter was replaced by another medical rescue unit. Two crew members came down and efficiently strapped the girls onto stretchers so they could be hoisted to safety. Then they helped Brian into a harness, and once he was aboard, they followed, and the helicopter sharply turned, rose, and was on its way.

Only when they were speeding toward the hospital did Brian realize how exhausted he was. He tried to lift his arm during a conversation with a medic and found it wouldn't cooperate but only dropped back into his lap aching dully.

The medic chuckled. "You work on 'em so long without even thinking about it; then your muscles just sort of quit on you. You'll be a little sore for a day or so," he said and then lapsed into a story of a difficult rescue that made the travel time pass very quickly.

At the hospital, Violet and Carl were already standing in the parking lot with Greg and Rit when the second helicopter landed. Bunny had fully awakened, and she smiled broadly at her friends as she and her sister were transferred onto flat gurneys and were wheeled toward the emergency entrance.

After they took the still unconscious Grace into a treatment room, Violet spoke quietly with Bunny, holding her cold fingers in her warm hands. "Bunny, when you were taken captive, we decided to look through your things." She paused, glancing at Carl, who stood close beside them. "I hope you don't feel it was an invasion of your privacy. Somehow I felt that this morning was the time for that sketch you've been keeping so private to be revealed." She paused again as Bunny's eyes twinkled with understanding. "When we saw what you drew, we immediately contacted the authorities, but it was hard to convince them to act on the merits of the drawing alone. They did respond by coming out to the cabin, though, and when they heard everything we had to say, they called a rescue unit in."

Carl chimed in to pass along more of the story. "And wouldn't you know they'd find the culprits first and take them into custody. But it's probably a good thing they got to them when they did. They were probably having trouble keeping the snow off."

Coming into the waiting area, Rit looked around curiously. "Where's Greg?"

"And you are supposed to be a genius?" Brian gave him a friendly punch in the arm and tipped his head in the direction Grace had been taken.

The doctor joined them just then, pulling off his latex gloves. "She's coming around. Are there relatives?" Everyone pointed at Bunny, and he continued, "She dislocated her shoulder, but no bones were broken, and there does not appear to have been any head or spinal injury. After we warmed her up and got her onto IV fluids, she regained consciousness. We've taken care of the shoulder and given her a painkiller, and her vital signs are stable. And there's no frostbite. So, after some rest, your—"

Everyone chimed in, "Sister."

"Your sister should be just fine. We'd like to keep her and run some routine tests." At Bunny's nod of assent, he turned, briskly saying over his shoulder, "You're next."

As the doctor went back to the desk to record his notes, Carl spoke thoughtfully. "We have a very wonderful group of young people here, Violet." He paused before continuing. "They seem to have been brought together for a special reason."

She agreed and, with an expression as if something had just jogged her memory, released Bunny's hand and bent down to reach into her bag. "I brought your drawing along, thinking it might continue to help in some way. Everything went smoothly, though. Would you like it back now?" Violet offered the paper to Bunny.

As Bunny stretched out her hand, Brian and Rit leaned in to see. The sketch portrayed an incredible likeness of Brian, Rit, and Greg on a narrow mountain ledge, with Grace prostrate far below, Bunny by her side, and very close to them, the shape of a heart in the snow.

Just then a nurse arrived to roll Bunny into a treatment room for her examination. As Violet stooped to retrieve her purse, intending to accompany her young friend, Rit spotted a large black car pulling into the parking lot. Two men in dark suits and trench coats got out and began walking toward the door. Almost simultaneously a van pulled into the lot from another direction and parked close to the building. An attractive young woman in slacks and a parka and a middle-aged man with mussed up hair stepped out of the van, the man dragging a large camera with him.

"Here we go again," Rit remarked dryly. Brian just shook his head.

"Okay, how about Florida now?" Carl asked his wife.

Violet rolled her eyes heavenward and followed the stretcher into the treatment room.

Greg approached the group. "We're going to Florida?"

Rit inclined his head toward the new arrivals, directing Greg's gaze. As Greg groaned, Brian asked, "What next?"

All four men stood thoughtfully silent.

"Will you guys give me a minute with these people?" Carl asked the young men. "Meet me in the cafeteria," he instructed as the reporters and the government men rapidly approached the big sliding doors. Squaring his wide shoulders and facing the door with arms akimbo, he looked as immovable as a roadblock.

⋈ | ⋈

The three young men sat around a table off to the side of the cafeteria, each with a warm beverage steaming in front of him but no one partaking. They were seated thus for several minutes, looking like figures in a wax museum.

"What a sorry lot!" The playful insult rang out in the nearly empty room.

"Mr. Big!" Rit started to get up, but his shoelace had become caught in the crossed legs of the cafeteria chair, making him lose his balance and sit back down abruptly. "Did you get rid of them?" He asked, unfazed.

"For now," was the taciturn reply, and as everyone registered concern at his tone, Carl continued, "Oh, I'm not upset with *you* guys. I'm just sure both of those branches of society will keep flapping around us. I also found out that the terrorists who kidnapped the people your mother knew have killed one of the hostages. I'm sorry, Brian."

Brian bowed his head, pressing both thumbs against the bridge of his nose. "I think I should make a phone call. Excuse me, please." He rose and made a hasty exit.

"That leaves us to plan our next move." The big, former police officer's normally jovial features conveyed unusual seriousness. They were still brainstorming when Brian returned.

"What have you gentlemen decided while I was gone?" Brian asked politely.

Rit raised his eyebrows, Greg gave a negative shake of his head, and Mr. Big pursed his lips, narrowing his eyes pensively.

"Okay, what ideas are on the table?"

They reiterated the best thoughts that had come out of the discussion, but there was a general feeling of dissatisfaction. "Look. We're all worn out, so why don't you guys go get some sleep, and we'll pick this up tomorrow," Carl suggested with a long sigh.

"Dad, no disrespect, but I still have a problem with leaving Grace and Bunny here at the hospital."

"Son, I'll stay, and you can take these fellows and your mother back to the cabin."

"I think we should all stick together, sir," Brian said. "Just my opinion."

Carl held his hands out in an exasperated gesture; they had gone around the issues unsuccessfully again.

When Greg spoke, it wasn't to the other men. "God, we need a plan," he said simply. "We need your help, Jesus." He was weary, more so than ever before in his life. His body was fatigued, his mind and heart disillusioned, and he didn't foresee a happy ending. The terrorists wouldn't give up, the news people probably wouldn't either, and the government agency that was tracking the terrorist activity definitely wouldn't quit.

Violet walked into the cafeteria with the doctor. "The girls are in their room resting now. Bunny checked out just fine," she said, smiling until she observed the men's troubled faces. Her smile quickly faded.

"I'm glad you're here, doctor," Carl began as he moved to his wife's side. "We have a problem, and since it may involve the hospital staff, I believe you ought to know about it." He proceeded to fill the doctor in on the dilemma they were facing, including the difference of opinion regarding the division of the group.

When he got to this point, the doctor interrupted. "Splitting up your party won't be necessary. We have large families living in these mountains that stay right here with their loved ones, even for several days at a time. You've seen what the weather can do around here. Besides, I have a professional interest in your stay." They all looked at him, nonplussed. Singling out Rit, Brian, and Greg, he explained. "I understand that you three men were battling the elements today, and I'd like to check you out."

The young men began to mutter objections and professions of excellent health, but the doctor waved the protests away with an authoritative hand, and they ended up following him like little children to the exam rooms.

⇥|⇤

Violet and Carl conferred for a while longer in the cafeteria, and then stopping briefly at the nurses' station to find out where they were to be situated for the night, they continued down the corridor to locate the girls. Peeking into the dimly lit room, they viewed the peacefully slumbering sisters with tenderness.

"We almost lost them, Violet." The big man's voice cracked. She gazed at their innocent faces wordlessly, a great thankfulness welling up in her heart at God's merciful intervention. Pulling the door closed, they quietly backed out into the hallway and entered the next room down.

After taking off her shoes, Violet stretched out on one of the neatly made hospital beds. She sat back up after a moment, just to reach a corner of the lightweight blanket folded up at the foot of the bed before lying back down and covering most of herself as her eyes closed.

Before her husband even turned around, she'd drifted off to sleep.

"My sweet Violet," he whispered as he looked at her. "My love for you increases every year that goes by."

Carl discovered, as he began unwinding from the high-pressure day, that his arm was aching. He stiffly reached inside the neck of his shirt and drew out the sling he'd pushed out of the way earlier, tucking his arm into it. Then he lay down and stretched his long legs out on the bed across from his wife.

"The three musketeers," as the nurses called them, were assigned to the room on the other side of the sisters'.

As they settled in, Rit's voice came out of the shadows. "Do you think there will be more of those scary dudes coming after Bunny?"

"Yes." Greg's tone was still tired but contained a note of renewed faith instead of the fear that had been encroaching earlier. "They'll come back again, but God will give us a plan."

"Do you think the president got the sketches?" Rit questioned from the darkness again.

"No." Brian answered this time. "My folks would have heard something about it. We may have to come up with a different way to get those drawings and our personal endorsements to him."

"So do we ask God for two plans or just one big plan?" This time the answer was in the form of a barrage of pillows flying through the dark room, all landing on Rit and his bed.

A spike of light suddenly slanted across the dimness as a nurse's silhouette appeared in the door. "Everything okay in here, gentlemen?"

Rit puffed up all the pillows around him, lying back with his fingers interlaced behind his head. "Yeah. These guys are real nice guys. Look, they gave me all their pillows so I would be comfortable tonight." After the door shut again, muted jovial objections could be faintly heard, but in a short while, there was only the deep silence of people sleeping, waiting.

28

Rit heard singing coming out of the silence from a short distance away. He sat up listening more closely and then slowly got out of bed to discover the source of the beautiful sound. Opening the door, he stepped into the hazy corridor. There were many other doors to choose from. He listened at each one, moving from one side of the corridor to the other, until he located the one with the singing. He gave the door a light nudge, and it opened easily. He slipped silently into the room.

There he saw the golden girl of his dreams again, this time sitting on the bank of a river, her curly, blonde head of hair tipped to one side as she sang a song almost too wonderful for him to bear. Someone else was there with her, but even without being able to see the other person, Rit knew *that* person was the reason Bunny was capable of using her voice. It could have been unsettling, like a scene from a sci-fi movie, but instead Rit found just staying on his feet was difficult because of the overwhelming power of love in that place. He felt rooted to the spot. He wanted to stay there forever and enjoy the presence of so much love, listening to the heavenly music. Love was holding him in place, lifting his spirits and giving him peace about the past and future all at the same time.

⇥|⇤

Brian heard a song in his soul while he slept. The song was so clear that he awoke with the words in perfect order in his consciousness. He tiptoed out of the room into the hallway and headed toward the nurses' station.

As he approached, the solitary little nurse, deeply involved in her work on the computer in front of her, jumped two inches in her chair and swiveled quickly around to face him. "I didn't expect anyone to be up yet. Can I help you?" she inquired, gathering her composure.

"I'm sorry. I didn't mean to startle you. I only wanted to ask whether you have a pen and piece of paper I could have, please. I woke up thinking of something, and I'd like to write it down," Brian politely explained. He smiled down at her as she bent to pull the printer drawer open.

"Computer paper okay?" she asked as she pulled several pieces out and handed a pen from the desk to Brian along with the paper.

"Fine, thanks," he answered, and with another smile and a glance at the clock above her head, Brian walked across the hall to the small waiting room, now lit only by an aquarium and a dim table lamp. He settled into a chair near the lamp and felt around for the switch. "Yes," he said under his breath as the switch proved to be three-way, providing brighter light. "How did it go? Oh yes, I think it started like this…"

He put pen to paper and didn't stop writing until, with a deep sigh, he leaned back, pulling the paper to his chest. He tipped his head back against the wall behind the chair, and closing his eyes in thought, fell asleep again right where he was.

Violet began to stir restlessly in her sleep, eventually waking herself up by sensing the loss of her pillow, pushed out of the bed by her restive turning.

"Well, you're up early," a deep voice from the next bed spoke.

"There's no bed like home," came the sleepy reply, accompanied by a deep yawn.

"Wonder how their coffee pot works."

"Shall we try to find it?" Two shadowy figures bumped into each other as they got out of bed and converged in the center of the room. A muffled chuckle and a soft laugh floated out into the hallway followed by the people belonging to the voices as they emerged in their rumpled clothes.

"This nose can always find the coffee pot. Follow me," Carl said.

"I always do dear." Violet tucked her arm under his, and they ambled contentedly down the hall toward the elevator.

Bunny's eyes popped open and shifted immediately toward the silhouette of her sister in the bed parallel to hers. She stared hard in the half-light, trying to see whether Grace's chest was rising and falling or still. Unable to tell in the dim light, she jumped from her bed, pulling loose the finger monitor she hadn't even noticed was there. A low beeping started and immediately brought a nurse to the room with a question that Bunny couldn't answer.

She was standing with the light from the hallway shining on her face, looking like a deer caught in car headlights, when Grace awakened from her deep sleep and discerned what was happening. Grace started to speak, but little except a croak came out. She began clearing her throat over and over, beginning again and again, but she had been chilled so thoroughly in her snowy adventure the day before that she couldn't speak either. Clearing her throat like an old car trying to get started, she waved her hands in a consoling gesture toward Bunny, who was looking relieved and panicked at the same time—relieved because Grace was alive, panicked because she was afraid that her sister would now also be unable to speak. Although the memory of a feeble whisper on the day of their snowy drama lingered, Bunny knew deep in her heart that her own will was not enough to bring back her own voice. Now her eyes focused with deep concern on Grace's struggle.

⇥|⇤

The unaccustomed sound of beeping with an accompanying gurgling, choking noise caused Greg to sit up suddenly. "What is that? Is someone dying?"

"This is a hospital. Why did you wake me up, man? I wanted to stay there, it...she…it was all so wonderful!" Rit's hair was standing straight up on his head, making him look cranky.

"What do you mean, this is a hospital?"

"Well, people die in hospitals."

"Great morning thought, bro." Greg shook his head in mock disgust. "I thought I heard it coming from the next room down—the girl's room."

Without further exchange, two pairs of feet hit the cool floor, and the young men rushed from their room toward the next one. They flung the partially closed door wide open to see Bunny still hovering with concern in the center of the room while the nurse poured water from a little Styrofoam pitcher and handed it to Grace, who continued to choke a bit.

"I don't think you gentlemen should enter a hospital room without knocking first," the nurse said flatly.

"Oops!" Red spun around to present his back to the scene in the room.

Greg just bashfully lowered his eyes. "Sorry."

Grace laughed, finally clearing her throat. "Come in," she invited in a still shaky tone.

Bunny sat on the edge of her bed, swinging her feet in comfortable relief.

The nurse puffed her cheeks, blowing air slowly through pursed lips. "Okay, you guys can visit for a while, but the doctor will be doing rounds soon." She bustled out, closing the door with a soft thud.

The four young people looked at each other in silence. Grace patted the bed for Greg to sit beside her, and he moved quickly to her side, enveloping her in a big, long embrace, expressing all his relief and gratitude for her rescue and recovery in that simple gesture.

The doctor's brief check-up interrupted the reunion, but when he left to begin the discharge process, the two young men went straight back into the room. Bunny had gathered up the clothes and effects that Violet had brought from the cabin and was carrying them into the adjoining bathroom. She reemerged in a few minutes, clothed and with wild curls combed. She motioned for Rit to leave with her as she pulled on the door.

As they wandered into the hallway, Rit asked, "Hey, would you mind if I change too? Then maybe we can find some breakfast." At Bunny's nod, he stopped off at his room, reappearing shortly in fresh clothes and with his hair hastily tamed. They continued down the hallway until Bunny happened to notice Brian still sitting in the small waiting room, his head tipped back against the wall and softly snoring. She pointed and smiled with her eyebrows arched high in a mischievous questioning look.

Rit tiptoed over to Brian, took the pen now held loosely in one hand, and with great care, balanced it gently behind Brian's ear. The pen actually stayed there for the minute it took to sink into Brian's subconscious that there was something odd being done to him. With eyes still closed, he lightly swatted his ear, which caused the pen to fall down his chest.

Brian opened his eyes slowly, focusing first down his front, to see what had disturbed him, and then spotting Rit and Bunny out of the corner of his eye. "How can you think of things to annoy people so early in the morning, Rit ?"

Bunny made motions, pointing at herself, holding her hands spread out before her innocently.

"Oh, you want me to think it was you who thought of this, Bunny? No, I don't think so."

Bunny wrinkled her nose at him and waved for Brian to join them. Picking the pen up, he tapped it on the arm of the chair thoughtfully, looking over her head at Rit, and then said, "Give me about twenty minutes, okay? Are you going to the cafeteria?" At his confirmation, he continued, "I'll meet you down there. Don't hold breakfast for me, though. Is everyone all right this morning?"

Rit answered that Greg was with a recovering Grace and that they hadn't seen Greg's parents yet, then with a respectful nod, he and Bunny moved off toward the elevator.

Violet and Carl were heavily involved in a serious conversation when Rit and Bunny entered the cafeteria. To the young people, it looked like the Johnsons were engaged in plans of the direst nature. Carl kept drawing on the table with his pointer finger, and sometimes Violet would nod, while at other times she would seem to erase the table drawing and use her gestures to convey something else.

Rit nodded his head toward the serving counter, drawing Bunny's attention to the matter of getting breakfast before moving again to join the older couple.

Violet spotted them standing indecisively about ten feet away, trays in hand, and with a sudden smile crossing her face, she called out to them to sit at the same table. The conversation then shifted to small talk suitable for the arrival of still slightly sleepy teenagers, and everyone continued talking amicably until Brian showed up, neat and clean and bearing a tray of food as well. Conversation paused for smiles all around, and

Violet patted the place next to her. When Brian was seated, they all continued chatting until Greg walked in, supporting Grace with one hand and carrying a tray loaded with food for two in the other. The light conversation broadened again to include the last two of the group until everyone had finished eating. Then an uncomfortable silence ensued.

Oddly, it was Bunny who asked an opening question in her own way. Leaning into the center of the table to get everyone's attention, she made eye contact with each one. Then slowly turning her palms upward, she made circles outward in an interpretable gesture meaning, "What do we do now?"

Carl took a deep breath. Planting his elbows on the table with clasped hands, he bowed his head on his hands, peering over his knuckles into the eyes of his wife. She silently shook her head, indicating that they hadn't come to a satisfactory conclusion.

Brian spoke into the growing heaviness. "This is maybe off the subject, but I had the strangest experience last night."

Violet, feeling a change of subject might be very good, looked at him encouragingly. "Tell us about it, Brian."

He shifted a little on his chair. "I heard a song in my sleep."

Rit looked at him sharply, remembering the lovely song of his own dream, but didn't say anything, allowing Brian to continue.

"I wrote down all the words when I woke up. When I was a little child, I used to make up songs about things

I saw around me or things that happened during the day, but as I grew older, I quit singing those little tunes. I don't remember ever thinking up a song while I slept."

Violet reached out her hand to lay it gently over Brian's. "Would you mind singing it for us?"

"Well...I..." Brian stuttered.

"If it wouldn't make you feel too awkward, maybe a song is just what we need," Violet persisted.

"Well...okay. It goes something like—" Brian began singing softly, his voice hesitant at first but then growing steadier.

> The other day I was walking in the rain.
> I met a man in a long gown at the side of the road.
> He said, "Do you know where you're going?"
> He said, "Son, do you want me to show you the right
>   road?"
> Well, of course, I wanted to know the best road to tread,
> So I said, "Sure, you just point the way."
> So he pointed to a narrow, hidden road.
> I said, "Sir, are you sure that's the road I should follow?"
> And he told me, "It isn't important where your feet fall.
> It only matters where you're going most of all,
> And it isn't the pain and the toil on the way—
> You're going to be with your Lord this way."
> The rain was cold, I was getting wet, and miserably I said,
> "I can't travel that hard road today, maybe a sunny day
>   instead."
> He lifted his kind eyes as I passed him by.
> He said, "Son, if you need somebody bad sometime, just
>   call me,
> Because it isn't important where your feet fall.
> It only matters where you're going most of all,

And it isn't the pain and the toil on the way,
You're going to be with your Lord that way."
The road I went was easy and wide, but the rain never quit.
I met another man, who said at the end I'd get dried off
    real quick,
And when he laughed, I felt somehow he was laughing
    at me.
The thought of what he said made me uneasy.
All alone and lost and hurt, I called my friend.
Suddenly there he stood before me.
I fell to my knees and prayed, "Lord, help me please."
He said, "Son, you did the right thing, now just follow
    me,
Because it isn't important where your feet fall.
It only matters where you're going most of all,
And it isn't the pain and the toil on the way,
You're going to be with your Lord this way."

Brian's voice drifted off on the last notes of the song, and everyone stared at him in a surprised way until Carl broke the silence.

"You can write pretty good music, can't you?"

Brian ducked his head modestly while the large man continued.

"God's gifts just keep on showing up right when we need them. I was feeling that we needed to come up with a failsafe plan right now and implement it immediately, but now that I heard that brand new song right off the heavenly press, I favor a different direction."

All eyes were on him. Even his wife had no idea what he would suggest.

"It's obvious that danger is stalking us. In a broader sense, danger is stalking our whole nation. And in a larger sense still, danger is stalking all the innocent of the earth. We have felt responsibility and tried to implement a plan to help our nation's leader get pertinent information. We continue to be at risk because of this decision, but what we can rely on is that nothing has happened by coincidence, and we form a powerful team under God that can effectively help the world we live in if we continue to submit our gifts to God's plan. I say we wait for God to tell us what to do next."

When he made this last statement, everyone sat quietly for a moment, taking in his words. Finally, one by one, a quiet smile came to each face, and they all slowly nodded their heads, looking around the table at their companions.

Carl rose to his feet. "How about we get our gear and head back to the cabin so we can find out what that plan is?"

The rest of the little group rose as one body with one purpose. Their footsteps and voices echoed and faded down the antiseptic hallways as they eagerly stepped into the next phase of their adventure, completely assured of divine guidance and love.